To my beautiful girlfriend, who asked for a silly trope with a happy ending.

D1109317

Prologue

Everything came to a head on the night of our school's Winter Formal, ironically. I guess I should've expected it, given that the plot of every teen movie ever seems to build into a climax that falls on the date of some sort of "important" school dance, but I honestly didn't see it coming. At least not until I was there, standing in front of a crowd of students with Sarah's hand in mine. I could feel a boulder-sized lump in my throat that wouldn't disappear no matter how many times I swallowed, and I knew she could feel how clammy my palm was.

Mr. Crenshaw, our school principal, stood onstage in front of us, along with several other pairs of students who were up for Winter Formal

King and Queen, because apparently that was a thing that our school actually did. Or... I guess it'd be Queen and Queen if me and Sarah turned out to be the winners. Which we probably would, even though Sam and Christine were pretty decent contenders as well. But there were a lot of people who'd voted for us. Most of them thought it'd be funny to give it to two girls, and the scattered giggles in the crowd as everyone waited for Principal Crenshaw to read out the names of the winners only made that more obvious.

Still, there were others out there who wanted us to win because it meant something. Because it would prove that things had changed for them. For us. What they didn't know was that we weren't really an "us". At least not in the way they thought we were. We would never be exactly what we'd pretended to be, regardless of what happened after tonight.

Sarah squeezed my hand and I didn't look at her. I was dreading Principal Crenshaw's winner announcement, because the winners had the option of giving a small speech. And Sarah was, frankly, about to blow our cover. I felt sicker by the second.

We didn't exactly attend the most open-minded high school. There were people who'd liked Sarah and me at the beginning of the school year and hated us now, just a few months later. But, fortunately, there were also people who'd used to feel neutral toward us and now loved us. And amongst those, there were people whose lives we'd changed. Those were the ones she was going to hurt tonight. Nevermind that she wasn't even doing it in the spirit of being honest. She was doing it because if she didn't tell, Christine would.

I shifted uncomfortably and released her hand, acutely aware of the hundreds of eyes on us as Principal Crenshaw opened the envelope in his hand. He paused for suspense, and I only took pleasure in the brief flash of disappointment visible on his face for a moment before he leaned into a microphone to call out, "Sarah Cooper and Katie Hammontree!"

The crowd in front of us erupted into a strange mixture of cheers and wolf-whistles and laughter as a couple of girls from the dance committee came forward to place a crown on each of our heads. They seemed confused at first when it came to which crown should go where, and so I ended up with an oversized King crown that I knew had to look out of place on my head. Even as the applause continued, I leaned in toward Sarah and tried to reassure her, "You'll do fine. I love you."

She gave me a nod and stepped away from me, accepting the microphone from Principal Crenshaw and taking her place front and center stage. I grit my teeth and took a step back, hardly able to fathom that she was really going to bite the bullet and do this now, with a quarter of our high school's student body watching her. Everyone was going to hate us. A lot of people were going to get hurt. Jake would probably never speak to us again.

But we also probably deserved it after what we'd done.

"I want to thank those of you that voted for us because you thought we deserved it," she began, shooting me a sideways look even as a guy at the front of the crowd whistled at us. My stomach twisted into a knot.

"There are a lot of people who wanted us to win this for the right reasons. And I know there are also a lot of people who probably just think this is funny and find it hilarious that that crown is way too big for Katie's head." There were some chuckles at that, and the same guy who'd whistled before shouted to us that we were hot together, which led to more laughter. A few months ago, Sarah'd have laughed too, but now she just let out a sigh.

"Look, what I'm trying to say here is that there's something I need to take some time to explain to everyone."

I heard her gulp, and she moved the microphone too close to her mouth. A shrill, piercing noise echoed around the gym, making more than a few people cringe. "Sorry. Um..." She paused again, and then took a deep breath and collected herself. I saw her straighten up and look out at the crowd, her gaze firm. She had her mind set on doing this, and when Sarah was set on achieving something, there was no talking her out of it.

"Alright. Here's the thing: It's true that I'm here at this dance tonight with someone I love. I care about Katie more than anything or anyone, and she knows that. She knows how I feel about her." She swallowed hard and looked back at me, but I could barely meet her eyes. What she said was true, but it didn't make this any easier to watch her do.

"But we weren't completely honest with everyone," she continued. Her voice – shaky but determined – echoed out across the gym, and her admission brought complete silence to the entire room. No one was laughing anymore. And as I looked out at the crowd, I saw no friendly faces.

She forced herself to press on.

"I was ignorant and immature and really, really stupid when all of this started just a few months ago, and I wanted attention from someone who it took me way too long to realize I meant nothing to. It was really, *really* dumb, and it was all completely my idea. I talked Katie into... into acting like we were a couple even though we weren't."

The silence was deafening. I felt my heart pound so hard in my chest it almost hurt, and if *I* felt this way about what she was saying, I couldn't fathom what Sarah was feeling.

"We never were a couple," she continued. "Not in the way we told everyone we were. We didn't spend our formative years dealing with sexuality crises, and I never really thought about dating Katie until this whole thing started. We faked all of it, and I know there's nothing I can say that will change how much hearing that hurts some of you. All I can say is that I'm sorry, and ask that you give me the chance now to explain what really happened."

My eyes were on Jake when she paused to let that sink in, and I'll never forget the look on his face right then. He was devastated and humiliated and betrayed and everything I'd been afraid he'd be. And as Sarah forced herself to keep going – to, evidently, tell the entirety of the senior class our story – I thought about the first day I'd ever spoken to Jake, just three months ago. The day that'd started it all.

The beginning.

Chapter One

Our town in Flowery Branch, Georgia looked a lot like it sounded. In the spring, when everything was alive and blooming, it was beautiful. In the fall, it was cold and windy, but there was about a two-week period in September where the leaves were orange, red, and brown, but hadn't fallen off of the trees yet. It was beautiful then, too, and I remember exactly when I met Jake because I stumbled upon him while I was walking home from school, admiring those leaves on our first day back at Flowery Branch High after Fall Break.

I walked home most days, unless I went home with Sarah. She lived close to our school and only had a five-minute drive every day, but I lived even closer, and had a ten-minute walk. It wasn't often that I ran into anyone on my way home, but that day was different.

I hadn't known Jake. I hadn't even recognized him from our school hallways or from sharing classes. It was like he was invisible until he was right in front of me, getting the contents of his backpack dumped out onto the sidewalk as he watched from where he'd been pushed to the ground.

Standing above him was Brett Larson, this kid that'd been a linebacker for our school football team until he'd recently gotten caught with tobacco. Now he was suspended, and, apparently, he was spending his recreational time picking on other kids.

I don't really know what made me stand up for Jake that day, but I did it. Maybe it was that it was the right thing to do. But there were other times in my life where I'd had the opportunity to do the right thing and then hadn't. Maybe it was just because I still really hated Brett for the time I'd caught him copying my homework answers in the third grade. Or maybe my instincts had just taken over.

I paused on the sidewalk, taking in Jake sprawled out on the ground with a bloody lip while a laughing Brett watched notebooks and pencils and a calculator spill out onto the ground, and then

I reacted, clenching my fists at my sides and storming up to Brett. "Hey! Leave him alone!"

Brett paused, saw me, and the smile disappeared from his lips. He tossed the backpack aside, into Jake's lap, and then rolled his eyes at me. "How about you mind your own business, Katie?"

"I take this way home every day," I bit out. "So if you're doing your bullying on this sidewalk, it's my business. Of course, you could keep going, if you want... but I'm sure Coach Collins would hate hearing about it. How long is your suspension again?" I pretended to tap my chin thoughtfully. "I wonder how long a second one would last?"

"Whatever." He shook his head at me, but I could tell he was backing off, and that was what mattered. "I should've known you were a queer, too."

"Charming," I countered, raising a middle finger in his direction as he turned and stalked away. My focus went to Jake, next, who shot me an appreciative look as I offered him a hand.

"Thanks. He's been hounding me for a while now." He got to his feet with my help and then bent down to start to gather his things. I tried to kneel to help, but he waved me away. "Don't worry about it. I've got it."

"Okay." I watched him, concerned, as he stuffed several notebooks back into his backpack, and tried not to stare too much at his lip.

Jake was skinny, almost overly so, and had glasses that were a little too big for him, but he was kind of a good-looking guy. His hair was carefully styled and he had this almost overly rosy-cheeked look that made him appear to be a little younger than he was. Initially, I mistook him for a freshman or a sophomore. "So why won't he leave you alone?" I asked, although Brett's parting comment had given it away.

Jake gave a bitter laugh as he zipped his backpack up. "Ah, you know, the gay thing. They say it gets better, though."

"People still tease other people for being gay?" I asked, arching an eyebrow. "That seems a little archaic. I thought it only happened in, like, rural Mississippi."

"Rural Mississippi and small-town Georgia, apparently," he replied with a tilt of his head. "Anyway, I should get going. I've got kind of a long walk today. Thanks again, seriously. No one's ever really stood up for me before."

He started to turn and walk away, but I fell into step beside him, not ready to finish our conversation. "Wait. You don't normally walk?" I was confident he didn't. I'd have noticed him.

"Uh, no. I kind of wrecked my car over Fall Break and it's at the shop until tomorrow. I'm not a big fan of the bus and my parents don't get off work until five, so today I have to walk home. It should only be an hour or so; I'll get back around four."

"Shouldn't you get your lip fixed up as soon as possible?" I asked him. It really did look bad. Not stitches bad, but it was definitely swollen. "I live right down this street."

He started to reply, but my phone beeped in my purse and I reacted quickly. It was a text from Sarah, and it said: *"Home yet? I'm coming over!"*

I shot back a response and looked to Jake again, newly inspired. "My friend Sarah's coming over; she can fix you up," I insisted. "She's going to college for nursing next year, so she loves playing doctor any chance she gets." I paused and then colored when my wording sank in, noting that Jake was struggling to hold back a smile.

"I know Sarah," he told me. "Sarah Cooper. And that is a strangely accurate description of her."

"Playing nurse, I meant," I corrected hastily. "Treating injuries and that kind of stuff. She considers it practice."

He grinned, and let me off the hook. "I think I had Chem class with her last year."

"You're a senior?" I asked him, unable to hide my surprise.

He laughed. "Yeah. So are you, Katie."

I flushed hard again, embarrassed that he knew my name but I didn't know his. "Yeah. So... are you up for coming over, um...?"

"Jake," he told me, but he didn't seem offended. "I know you don't know me; it's cool. I don't talk to many people."

"Why not?" I asked. He seemed friendly enough.

"Well, I guess it's a little harder to make friends when you're gay in a town like this. You're always worried about each new person you have to tell, and you never know whether someone will hate you or take it in stride. It's like playing friendship Russian Roulette."

"It can't be *that* terrible here," I said. "I know a few gay kids at our school."

"Do you?" He arched an eyebrow.

"Yeah. There's, um..." I wracked my brain for a name. "Oh! That guy, Hunter-"

"He transferred," Jake cut me off.

"Really?"

"Yeah. Last year."

"Well... there's this girl in one of my classes that I'm pretty sure is gay. She doesn't talk much but-"

"She fits all the stereotypes?" he finished for me. I felt embarrassed again.

"I guess."

"You have to admit," he said, "that there are pretty much no notable gay students at our school. At all."

"Notable?" I echoed. It seemed like a strange word to use.

"You know... popular. A well-liked, friendly, totally normal guy or girl who's attracted to the same sex."

"Well, that could change," I suggested, even though I doubted it would. Jake was right. The few gay kids I *could* think of were a fringe group that only really spoke to each other. And I didn't really talk to any of them.

Sarah and I'd always been what she jokingly called "tier 2 populars" – never quite spending time with most of the jocks and cheerleaders, but we had a few mutual friends with those groups, and we were relatively well-known by our classmates. It was, in hindsight, unsurprising that Jake knew both of us but I didn't know him.

"Doubt it," he replied with a shake of his head. "But I'm glad we at least have some cool people around who'll stick up for us." He looked over at me, curious. "Why *did* you help me, exactly?"

I shrugged my shoulders. "It just seemed... like something I needed to do. Besides, I know what it's like to feel like an outsider."

"Really," he said. It sounded more like a thoughtful statement than a question, but I nodded anyway. It was true. Throughout my elementary and early middle school years, I'd been a little heavy in the weight department. For a while, Sarah was the only friend I'd had. But one eating disorder and a lot of therapy later, and I was now around average weight for my height, according to my doctor. The end didn't justify the means, but it did stop me from getting teased, and I was eating healthy now.

"Yeah," I told him. "You know, sometimes people are just stupid. You can't help that. You just have to be confident in yourself. That's what I do, anyway." We reached my house and I pointed, slowing to a stop. "This is me. Do you wanna come in?"

He looked back at me in a way I was wasn't used to being looked at. Like I was a problem he couldn't quite solve. Then he smirked. "Yeah, sure. Your friend'll be here soon, you said?"

"Yeah. My parents aren't home, so you don't have to worry about them hassling you about your lip or anything."

"Cool."

He followed me inside and together we took off our shoes and backpacks, leaving them by the front door while I showed him around. My house was comfortably sized, with three bedrooms and two and a half bathrooms. I was an only child; we used the spare bed for guests.

I showed Jake the half-bath so that he could wash away the blood, then took out my phone to text Sarah again. *"Got you a patient,"* I told her, and it took her less than ten seconds to respond.

"Omg who???"

I didn't bother to tell her, because less than a minute later, she burst inside my house without knocking and threw her arms around me with a squeal. "Oh my God, I missed you!"

I laughed as I hugged her back, and we shared a grin once she'd pulled away. "You got a tan!" I noticed. She'd spent Fall Break on a cruise with her parents. Her father was a musician who performed on cruise liners for a living, so she pretty consistently got complimentary tickets. I'd been on a couple of trips with her family.

Sarah was an only child, too. She had the blue eyes of her mother and the dark hair of her father, and I'd always thought she was beautiful. Our parents liked to say that we complimented each other, given that I had a rare combination of brown eyes and blonde hair.

"I fried first," she told me with a shake of her head. "It was terrible. But it looks good now, right?"

"Gaw-geous!" I drawled, and that made her laugh as she wrapped her arms around me again.

We hugged, tightly, and she sighed out, "Jeez, I missed you. I wish we'd had a fourth ticket."

"It was boring here," I agreed, resting my chin on her shoulder. "Nothing to report."

"I have something," she told me abruptly, pulling away with a satisfied smirk. I heard a throat clear nearby and suddenly remembered Jake, who was now standing in the bathroom doorway, watching us both with two raised eyebrows.

"Am I interrupting something?"

Sarah jumped a little, then swiveled to face him. "Oh my God, you scared me!" She paused, then immediately moved to him. "Whoa, is your lip okay?"

"Brett Larson was messing with him. I saw them on my way home," I told her.

"Ugh," Sarah scoffed. "I hate that asshole." She spoke to Jake even as she ducked into the bathroom to get the first aid kit in the cabinet. "Did you know that when we were in third grade, he used to copy Katie's homework, like, every day?"

"Every day," I repeated matter-of-factly, watching Jake with some amusement as Sarah doted on him. He seemed a little overwhelmed by how high-energy she was. I was used to it by now.

"So what'd you do? Step into his line of sight?" Sarah joked. "What's your name, anyway?"

"Jake," I answered for him, given that Sarah was tending to his lip at the moment. "You guys had Chem together."

"Really?" Sarah raised an eyebrow. "Oh. Well, I probably just don't remember you because it took every single ounce of concentration I had just to pass that class. I'm terrible at science. Got a B-minus though because I study hard, unlike this one." She pointed over her shoulder at me with a thumb and shot me a smile, and then stepped back a moment later to admire her handiwork. "There. All cleaned up."

"Thanks." Jake tapped at his lip, wincing a little, and then looked between us for a moment. "So... you guys are pretty close, then? I mean, I've heard your names mentioned together a lot, so I figured you were friends, but..."

"We're the best of friends," Sarah cut in matter of factly, wrapping an arm around me and pulling me to her. "I almost died without her this break, you have no idea."

"Huh." He looked back and forth between us for another moment. "That's cool, I guess. I don't think I've ever had a friend like that before."

"Well, we've grown up together," I explained. "Like sisters."

"Closer than sisters," Sarah corrected proudly. "Sometimes we even finish each other's sentences."

"Yeah?" He raised an eyebrow again, and then looked over his shoulder abruptly. "So Katie, do you think I could grab a glass of water?"

"Oh, yeah, sure. The cups are in the cabinet above the dishwasher."

"Thanks."

He left the room for a moment, heading into the kitchen, and Sarah immediately turned to face me. She spoke under her breath even as she shot me a warning look. "He seems nice. But you're not into him, are you?"

I let out a quick chuckle. "No. He's gay, anyway."

"Are you serious? I mean, I knew we had them at school, but I've never actually gotten to know one."

"Well, maybe we should," I suggested. "Like you said: He seems nice."

"I bet he'd go shopping with us," she replied, sounding enthused at the idea. I let out another laugh.

"Yeah. Maybe."

Jake came back a few seconds later, a glass of water in his hand, and for a moment, we all stood together in awkward silence. Finally, he cleared his throat.

"So... I don't know if I'm being too presumptuous... but there's this club I kind of belong to, and I thought, I guess... if you guys ever wanted more people to hang out with and talk to and stuff... or if you just wanted to hang out with me and talk, you could come. You know, if you felt like spending time with people who can relate to you. Everyone's really nice."

"Sure," I offered, just being polite, but Sarah looked at me as though Jake had just offered to pay for everything she wanted during her next trip to the mall.

"Wasn't I *just* saying before break that I need way more extracurriculars this year if I want to get into med school? We should do it!"

"Really?" Jake sounded surprised that she'd accepted his offer so quickly. "You think you can handle it?"

"I mean, we probably just do volunteer work and all that, right? How hard can it be?"

"Well-" Jake started to say, but he was interrupted by the sound of our garage door opening. "Shit, is that your parents?"

"Probably my mom," I admitted. "She won't mind that you're here, though."

"Well, I don't want to risk your parents trying to make me call mine or something when they see my lip. I'm gonna see if the swelling goes down before dinnertime tonight and hopefully work some magic with makeup. My older sister can help me." He moved to the front door and grabbed his backpack. "Thanks a lot, though. Both of you. If you're still interested tomorrow, meet me after school by the front office, okay?"

"We'll be there," Sarah agreed, and then he was gone. The front door slammed shut behind him, and she grinned at me the second we were alone. "Awesome. Now I just have to ace most of my classes this year."

"Shouldn't we have found out exactly what kind of club he's in first?" I asked.

23

"I mean, how bad can it be?" she retorted, crossing to the living room couch and taking a seat. "It's probably some science club or something, in which case we don't have to do anything because we'll just let everyone else do the work."

"What if it's like a gay thing?" I pointed out.

"We have a gay club?" Sarah's eyebrows furrowed uncertainly.

"I don't know. Do we?"

"I don't think so. If we do, I haven't heard about it."

"Well, what if we do, and it is? We're not gay."

"So?" She laughed. "You don't have to be gay to join a gay club."

"But people will think we're gay," I pointed out.

Sarah paused, looking uncertain again. "...You think so?"

"Of course, if we're in a club for gay people."

"We could be, like, allies or something. Besides, even if anyone did think we were gay, it's not like it'd be that bad, right? It's not exactly the end of the world."

"Not that bad," I deadpanned, taking a seat next to her. "Did you not just clean up a busted lip?"

"He's a guy," Sarah sighed out, as though I was missing something obvious. "It's not hard for girls like it is for guys, because straight guys think it's hot." She waved the topic away before I could respond, and abruptly changed the subject.

"Anyway, speaking of guys, here's my news. Sam texted me a couple of days ago. I think we might be close to officially 'talking' status soon."

I had to keep from groaning as she waited for my reaction. The thing about Sarah was that when she wanted something, she *really* wanted it, and although most things she wanted she seemed to not want for very long, there were two that were the exception to the rule. The first was to get into med school, which was the primary reason why despite seeming shallow to the majority of the student body, Sarah was actually a pretty hard worker, and why the most scared I'd ever seen her was last year when she'd been sure she was going to flunk her Chem class.

The second thing was Sam Heath. He was a football player at our school that Sarah'd been obsessed with since freshman year. Of course, she tended to jump from crush to crush pretty frequently, but for some reason Sam had stuck. Regardless of whom she was chasing during any given month, it was always understood that she'd be willing to drop any other guy the instant Sam gave her the time of day. I'd never understood it; he wasn't even that cute, and yet she'd tried to get his attention for the past four years. And failed. Well, up until now, anyway.

"Let me guess: He wanted to know if your English class had homework over the break?" I asked.

"Oh my God, shut up," she whined, punching my shoulder lightly. "You're supposed to be happy for me! This is a serious breakthrough."

"Don't you think that if he liked you he'd have already tried dating you by now?" I pointed out.

"Not when he's got a dozen other girls waiting around for him to notice them, too," countered Sarah.

"And now he's finally gotten around to you. Sounds like true love."

She scoffed. "You're so cynical. Are you gonna be like this forever now just because it didn't work out with you and Austin?"

"All I'm saying is that maybe you should look for someone who thinks you're special without all of the extra effort from you."

"No guy thinks like that," Sarah dismissed. "I'm one dramatic gesture away from a date with Sam; I can feel it. I just need something to help me stand out."

I sighed quietly. She was hopeless sometimes. "Suit yourself. But I'm not funding the chocolate binge when it doesn't work out."

"Fair enough." She bit her lip and smiled, excitement radiating from her in waves. "I can feel it. This year is gonna be special."

"Oh, is it now?" came my mom's voice from the hallway that led to the garage. We both turned to watch her enter the living room and set her purse down on the coffee table. "And why is that?" she asked. I could tell she was just teasing, but I answered anyway.

"Sarah's determined to hatch a plan to snag the guy she's been pining over for the past four years."

"The quarterback one?" Mom replied with surprise.

"He's a running back," Sarah corrected. "And he took the time to get my number from someone."

"Ooh, exciting. And what did he want to talk about?" My mother turned away from us to hang up her coat, but I glanced at Sarah in time to see her cheeks pink.

"I knew it!" I laughed out even as she went redder.

"Okay, we had this stupid journal thing for English. But it's progress!"

"You are so sad," I told her with a shake of my head. Mom looked amused by the both of us.

"Well, dating doesn't get any easier, girls. It's better you learn the ins and outs of it early on."

"Tell that to Katie," said Sarah. "How long has it been since you and Austin?"

"Just a couple months," I said, eager to change the subject. "That's not that bad. And anyway, you've never even dated Sam and four years later you're still not over him. You're way worse."

"I don't give up on the things I want. There's nothing wrong with that."

"There is when he probably doesn't even know your last name and you know what his favorite song is."

"Hush." She clapped a hand to my mouth, then cringed and yanked it away when I licked her palm. "Ew! Gross."

"You were asking for it."

"Sarah, are you staying for dinner?" Mom interrupted. She'd gone into the kitchen at some point, and now she peered out at us from the doorway.

"Oh, no, that's okay. I should get back soon. I just needed to recharge my Katie bar."

Mom nodded and disappeared back into the kitchen, and Sarah stood and went to go put her shoes back on. I followed behind her with an exaggerated sigh.

"So are you gonna ask Sam to catch you up on what you missed in class today?" I asked her. She'd only gotten home from her vacation around noon today, which meant she hadn't gone to school. We had six classes total, and I shared just a couple of them and then lunch with her. I wasn't, however, in her English class with Sam.

28

"Maybe I should. We'll see." Once she had her shoes on, she straightened up and faced me, arms outstretched toward me. "Hug for the road?"

I squeezed her tight and mumbled, "I missed you."

"Me too," she whispered back, and then she was waving goodbye to my mother and me and heading out through our front door.

After she left, I helped my mom cook dinner. That was kind of our thing. I loved cooking, and every day, my mom would go to work, I'd go to school, and then right after we both got home she'd start dinner and I'd help. Then my dad would arrive and we'd eat together as a family. And I liked that about my family. I liked being close with my parents, and I liked that I could tell them anything, particularly my mom. Aside from Sarah, she was my best friend.

Sarah's family was different. She lived in a house much bigger than mine, and frankly they were kind of loaded. It wasn't even because of her parents; her grandfather died around the time she was born and he was apparently very talented when it came to the stock market, so he left a lot of money behind.

Sarah lived in one of the nicest neighborhoods in Flowery Branch, but she also rarely saw her dad because of his job, and from what I'd seen growing up with her, her mom was a little disconnected, to say the least. She cared more about the next country club event than how her daughter'd done on her English test, and that was kind of sad to watch sometimes, especially given that I had two parents that cared so much about me. So *I* got a lot of parental quality time and bonding, and *Sarah* got free cruises and an empty house to throw parties in. I liked to think that my parents picked up a little of the slack, though. Sarah was over at my house so much anyway that we were like a second family to her.

My mom had a lot to say about the conversation we'd had in the living room as we cooked together. "You know, I remember being just as boy crazy at that age. I even had my own Sam."

"I'm guessing he wasn't Dad?" I asked, grinning. My dad was kind of a dork.

"Not even close." Mom laughed. "He was this big, hulky guy on the wrestling team. I think the line he used to use... oh, God..." She started laughing again as she recalled, "When I finally tried having an actual conversation with the guy, he told me how many times he thought he could bench press me, and I think my crush died in that moment."

"Ew!" I wrinkled my nose and shook my head even as I stirred noodles into a boiling pot of water.

"Right? Anyway, what I'm getting at is that those things rarely go the way we want them to. Mostly because you don't actually know the person, so you put this ideal version of them on a pedestal, and that's actually what you're falling for instead. And once you finally do get to know them, you like them even less than you'd have liked them if it had just never occurred to you to date them, because then they're just a disappointment when they're not exactly what you thought they'd be."

"Mom, preaching to the choir." I told her. "But you know how she gets. Once Sarah's set on something, she won't rest until she gets the outcome she wants."

"Well, I wish her the best of luck, but I have a feeling she's going to be greatly disappointed." Mom finished grabbing a second pot from the cabinet and opened a can of spaghetti sauce. "Anyway, is there something I don't know about what happened between you and Austin?"

I furrowed my eyebrows, wondering what on Earth had made her think that. "No, why?"

"Well, Sarah just mentioned it, and I know how things go. You tell your parents what you feel comfortable telling them and your friends get to hear the rest."

"No, she was just... being her," I deflected. "He and I are fine. Just not talking."

"Well, I'm still sorry to hear that. He was a really nice guy. I think he would've made a good friend."

"Yeah, me too. I don't think I get to decide if we stay friends or not, though. Not since I broke up with him."

"That's true." Mom brought the sauce to a simmer, and a while later, I helped set the table while she scooped out three plates of spaghetti and covered them with sauce.

Dad walked in through the garage door just as dinner was ready, tossing his coat over the couch and calling out, "Where are my girls?"

I rolled my eyes as Mom went to him and kissed him, and then I waited for him to hug me hello, like he always did. We sat down together moments later, and as we ate, Dad asked, "So how was your first day back? No Sarah today, right?"

"She wasn't at school, but she came over after and then left an hour or so ago," I explained.

"Ah. Of course." He chuckled as he rolled a pile of noodles onto his fork, and then asked, "So did anything interesting happen today?"

For a moment, I debated whether or not to tell them about Jake, but decided eventually to go ahead and say something. We'd talked about homosexuality before, and I think my parents were a huge part of why I'd never understood why gay people were bullied. My uncle was gay, and although he lived across the country and I'd only met him a few times, his existence meant that in my family, being gay was normal.

"Yeah, actually." I took another bite of my food as they waited for me to continue. "Um, there was this kid getting picked on on my way home. I saw him with this other guy from the football team; his lip was busted and everything. He said it was because he was gay."

"You're kidding," Mom cut in. "Is he okay?"

"Yeah." I nodded. "I actually let him come here and Sarah cleaned him up. But he pretty much left right when you got here. He was worried you'd try and get in contact with his parents."

"Well, we should certainly contact the school." Mom looked across the table to Dad. "Don't you think, Jeff?"

Dad's eyebrows furrowed as he chewed his food. Once he'd swallowed, he sighed. "I don't know. Maybe he wants to handle it himself."

"How can you say that, with your brother being the way he is?" Mom asked him. "Would you have let Kevin take that from another boy back when you two were kids?"

"Well, he did," Dad pointed out. "And much worse than it is today. His solution was to take up boxing." He grinned. "They left him alone after that."

"Well, not every gay child can just take up a violent sport to avoid getting bullied every day," Mom countered, clearly upset.

"I know. I'm just saying that if this kid avoided meeting you because he was worried you'd get his parents involved, he clearly wants to handle it himself. Besides, he obviously has someone he can count on now in our daughter." He smiled over at me, and Mom looked to me abruptly, almost like she'd forgotten I was even here.

"Oh, of course. Well, I'm just glad to be proven we raised you correctly," she said. "Good for you and Sarah."

"He invited us to join a club he's in," I told them. "He seems nice."

"Well, you could always use more friends," Dad said, and received a glare from Mom at that.

"What's that supposed to mean? The friends she has are just fine."

"I just mean it'd be nice to see some more friendly faces around!" Dad insisted. "Of course we love Sarah, but it was nice meeting Austin, too. I'd be happy to finally get to say hello to all of these kids you're hanging out with on a daily basis."

"It's not like that," I explained. "There's a different between friendship and having acquaintances. I have a lot of acquaintances. You know, the people that invite you to parties because you kind of have mutual friends but that you'll only actually talk to once a week or so?"

"All I got out of that is that you're going to parties," Dad replied. "What kind of parties?"

"Really crazy keggers," I told him, straight-faced. "I drank an entire bottle of vodka all by myself at the last one."

"Five out of ten for that one," he rated. "You'd have died if it were true."

"Aw, shucks," I sighed out. Mom watched the two of us, a smile on her lips.

"So how do you feel about joining this club?" she eventually asked. "It's a commitment."

"I mean, I guess it'd be fine if it doesn't have a meeting, like, every day or something," I decided. Then I shrugged. "I guess I'll hear more about it tomorrow."

Chapter Two

I slammed my locker door shut the next morning and immediately jumped when I felt something hard press into my shoulder. It turned out to be Sarah's forehead, and she stood up straight as I turned around to face her, a pout on her lips.

"I'm tired," she said.

"Were you up all night texting Sam?"

"Thinking of what to say," she corrected. "Him actually talking to me was the worst thing that's ever happened to me."

"That was a quick change of heart," I said as we turned to walk down the hallway together. A girl – Annie – that I used to talk to in my Trig class last year passed by us, and I raised a hand to wave at her. She smiled and waved back.

"It's not a change of heart," Sarah told me. "I just wish this was easier. Why is it so hard getting a boyfriend?"

I laughed at that. "It's not... at least not for you. Your problem is keeping one."

"Well, why is it so hard getting the one I'd actually want to keep?"

"Because life sucks," I told her as we entered our next class.

A boy named Colton who sat in the front row heard me, and quipped as we walked by, "That's a very cynical way of thinking about things, you know."

"She's a very cynical person, Colton," Sarah sighed out. "You should know this by now."

He grinned at us as we took our seats near the back. Once we had our notebooks out and were waiting for class to start, I let out a sigh and turned to face Sarah, reaching out to grip her hand with my own. She mirrored my actions dismally. "Look. I'll be completely honest with you. I don't think it's gonna work out."

"You sound like you're breaking up with me," she mumbled.

"Then just picture Sam saying those same words," I suggested, "because you are going to get your heart broken. This guy is your typical jock who'll date the hottest girl who gives him the time of day."

"I'm hot," Sarah defended.

I let out a quiet groan. She was really, *really* hopeless. "Okay then, Sarah. Do what you want."

"Wait, am I not hot?" she hissed to me. Our teacher had just entered the classroom and was beginning to lecture at the front of the room.

"Of course you're hot," I told her quietly, and rolled my eyes when the girl sitting closest to us turned to raise an eyebrow at the two of us. "Just... can we talk about this later?"

"Fine," she huffed, and we agreed to leave it until the next time we saw each other: Lunch.

We ate lunch with four other girls every day and a couple of guys. The girls were Hannah, Dina, Josephine, and Bonnie. Hannah was our only cheerleader friend, but she was nice enough, and was also the reason Sarah and I were invited to so many social events.

Dina and Josephine were a lot like Sarah and I in that they'd been best friends for a long time. They were friendly and down-to-earth and easy to talk to, and I liked them the most out of everyone in our little lunch group.

Bonnie, although she seemed nice, too, was pretty quiet, and I think she only sat with us because she was friends with Graham, who was by far the kinder of the two guys that joined us at our table every day. The other was Connor, who could be cool on the rare occasions when he wasn't being an ass. He only sat with us because he had a thing for Sarah. And Hannah. And sometimes me, whenever he was particularly down on himself after rejections from his top two choices.

They were mostly Sarah's friends, but I liked them okay. I was used to being around people who knew her better than they knew me. I'd always been a little shyer than her, and she'd always been the one everyone liked a little bit better. But that was okay with me, because Sarah needed to be liked, and I didn't necessarily feel like I needed it in the same way that she did. It had hurt a lot getting teased in middle school, but I had a thicker skin because of it. And if the worst criticism anyone had of me now was that I was only able to get popular because I was friends with Sarah, well, I was doing pretty well for myself, then.

Anyway, we didn't actually talk about Sam at lunch, mostly because for all of her obsessing over him, Sarah never talked much about him in front of anyone other than me. She didn't really share much about herself with any of our other friends, actually. We were all into talking about when the next group hangout was or who had just started dating whom or whatever the other latest gossip was, but there weren't very many genuine conversations about meaningful experiences or about what our feelings were. Or at least not the deep feelings, and even as shallow as Sarah's crush seemed, I knew she was embarrassed that she liked someone as much as she liked Sam.

All in all, that second day back at school was pretty uneventful, beyond Sarah getting some hope that Sam Heath would someday know her last name. Those seven hours from eight in the morning to three in the afternoon were as boring as they always were.

At three fifteen, however, well... shit kind of hit the fan.

I hadn't seen Jake in any of my classes and had therefore concluded that we didn't share any, and so the first time I saw him that day was when Sarah and I met him at the front office. On the way there, she told me, "So Jake's actually in one of my classes. He said 'hi' to me today and everyone kind of looked surprised when I answered. It was a little weird."

"People are stupid," I sighed out.

When we reached the front office, Jake greeted us, all smiles. "Wow, you guys came! I'm actually kind of surprised."

"Well, we said we would," Sarah replied. "So here we are."

Jake let out a breath, then shook his head, almost in amazement. "Okay. Wow. This is gonna change things a lot around here, you know that, right? C'mon." He beckoned us after him, and together, we followed him down the hallway.

"Okay?" Sarah said, confused, and we exchanged strange looks as we walked. Neither of us knew what he was talking about.

"The meeting's in room 405 every Tuesday," he explained. "So just once a week. But sometimes we do things after school on other days, to, you know, help the community."

"Cool," I chimed in, relaxing a little.

"Yeah, nothing wrong with a little volunteer work," Sarah agreed. "This'll be fun."

"And you're sure you're ready?" Jake asked, pausing abruptly outside a closed door and turning to face us. "This is it. I know it's a big step."

"Well, you're here to help, I'm sure," Sarah told him. I knew her well enough to sense the edge of sarcasm to her tone, but it was obvious Jake didn't catch it.

"Of course. I'm gonna be here for the both of you. I mean, especially after what you're doing for the rest of the gay kids at our school. Your coming out is gonna completely change what everyone thinks of us."

He turned away to open the door, and completely missed our reactions. Sarah's eyes widened and she immediately turned to look at me. My jaw dropped.

We recovered quickly when we realized Jake was about to face us again. "I'm gonna let them know we have two new members, and you guys come in when you're ready, alright?"

"Sounds great," Sarah replied before I could, and then Jake was gone, ducking into the room and cracking the door behind himself. Sarah and I immediately went back to gaping at each other, but I could tell she was also holding back a smile. "Oh my God. He thinks we're gay."

"He thinks we're a gay couple," I elaborated. There was a long silence, and then I echoed Sarah: "Oh my God."

She raised a hand to her still-gaping mouth, and immediately dissolved into giggles. Then she seemed to realize something, and stopped laughing. "Oh my God, Katie, we have to go with it."

"What? No!" I countered. "Are you crazy?"

"You have to trust me. Just do it. Say we're a couple, okay?"

"Why on Earth would I do that?" I asked, my voice climbing a few octaves higher. There was *no* way I was going to listen to her. There were so many things wrong with her idea that I couldn't have even begun to name them all in those few seconds we were out in the hallway.

"Because this kid is already in there telling them we're together anyway, so what do we have to lose?" she pointed out even as I stared at her, wide-eyed. "Look, just trust me. C'mon."

She grabbed at my arm and tugged me toward the door, and I barely got out a hissed "wait!" before her hand was abruptly in mine and she'd pulled me into the classroom. I stopped struggling.

A group of twelve or so students sat in a circle of chairs as Jake stood in the center, and all thirteen of them were staring at us: Sarah smiling proudly as her hand squeezed mine so tightly it was going numb, and me, clearly uncomfortable as I offered a meek wave with my free hand. "Hey."

The first one to speak was a girl with short, pink hair, who I'd later find out was named Hattie. "Ho...ly... shit," she said.

"Knew it," a boy I was surprised I recognized chimed in, and high-fived the guy next to him with glee. I suppressed an offended look. Knew it? What was *that* supposed to mean?

"Alright, so as you can see, guys, these two are our newest LAMBDA members," Jake finally said, trying to break the tension. "Katie-"

"Hammontree and Sarah Cooper, yeah, we know," another girl cut in. Jessa. She was eyeing us suspiciously. "You guys are actually together? Seriously?"

"Seriously," Sarah replied as I tried not to fume beside her. It was easy to see how big of a mess she'd already gotten us into. If we denied it now we'd just look like giant assholes. "Katie and I have been dating for about two months now, and we're ready to tell the world."

I grit my teeth and stayed quiet. In that moment, I honestly think I was angrier at Sarah than I'd ever been. She did a lot of stupid, impulsive things, but this took the cake. And while she was smooth-talking her way into the hearts of these people, I was thinking ahead. While we were sitting down in two empty chairs and she was beginning to tell some bullshit story about how she'd known since she was thirteen that she liked girls, I was realizing why she'd wanted to do this. And while she was telling them how she'd been in denial for a while about her feelings for me, I was realizing how irrevocably big this lie truly was.

And right around the time everyone was watching me expectantly, waiting for *my* story, I realized how much it was already going to hurt these people if we told them we were making it all up.

So as they stared at me in that circle, waiting for me to explain when I'd realized that I, too, liked girls, I swallowed hard, took a deep breath, and then began, "I guess I didn't know until recently..."

The meeting went on for a while, with almost everyone in noticeably higher spirits. They talked about what'd happened to Jake and how I'd stopped it, and he shared how he'd realized from the way I was talking and the way Sarah and I interacted that I was gay and that we were a couple. I obviously didn't have the heart to tell him he'd mistaken an eating disorder for homosexuality and close friendship for romance.

And when the hour was finally up and people were finally beginning to file out of the room, a girl named Violet who hadn't spoken much came up to us and told us, "You guys were really brave for coming here. I hope things really can change," and I had to bite my lip to keep from groaning because *how in the hell were we going to go back on this now?*

The girl named Jessa, meanwhile, brushed past Sarah close enough to give her a rather hard shoulder-check, and then turned back to roll her eyes in our direction even as she left the room. That was more than enough to tell us she wasn't buying it. She seemed to be the only one who felt that way, though.

We walked back with Jake to the parking lot, holding hands all the while even as he rambled on about how exciting it'd be to have openly gay popular kids and how we could do so much to help end gay bullying and maybe we could even win Prom Queens in April or at least Queens at the Winter Formal, and I felt sick by the time he left us. We got into Sarah's car so that she could give me a ride home, and I sat there in complete silence for what felt like hours. In reality, it was less than a minute before I finally said, "I think that was the shittiest thing I've ever done."

Beside me, she let out a sigh. "Oh, c'mon, Katie. Did you hear them in there? They were freaking out. And did you hear that one gay guy say we were adorable together?" She shot me a wink and I glared back at her. "Lighten up! I have a plan."

"What, to completely destroy the hopes and dreams of every gay kid at our school?" I countered. "That was sick. That was *so* mean, Sarah. We just lied!"

"But they don't have to know that," she explained. "Yes, it was a little rash, but I figured something out. Guys like lesbians, right? And they also like challenges."

"You-" I cut myself off to gape at her, fuming, and then shook my head. "I can't believe you."

"Look, I need to stand out to Sam somehow, and this puts the both of us on the map. You need to get back out there, Katie! I know seeing Austin moping around all the time is probably making you feel bad about dating again, but you both should move on, and this'll help you do that. And while we're at it, we'll be majorly boosting the confidence of the kids in that LGBT club. We're doing them a favor."

"And what happens when they find out the truth? Or are you just never expecting that to happen?"

"How will they find out? We'll just act like a couple until graduation, and then we'll fake a breakup and say we're bi, go back to guys, and then let everyone forget about it. No big deal."

"You are unbelievable."

"I know it's not the most foolproof plan, but it could work."

"It's completely selfish," I snapped. "You're doing all of this for a guy you hardly know! Okay, Sarah, what happens if it works and he... I don't know, falls for you, or whatever the hell you want. Then what? You 'cheat' on me with him? How do you explain supposedly only being attracted to women and then dating a guy?"

"I don't have to be a lesbian, then. I could just say I'm bisexual from the get-go."

"And then maybe you're no longer a challenge for Sam," I told her, crossing my arms. "So your plan's shot."

She was quiet for a moment, and I could see her confidence faltering a little. "Okay... so I didn't think about that."

"Yeah. You didn't think at all, I'd say," I bit back.

She let out a sigh. "Alright. I'm sorry I didn't think it through more. But we were kind of put on the spot. And hey, we wouldn't have been in the situation in the first place if you hadn't said whatever you did to Jake yesterday."

"I didn't say anything!"

"Well, clearly you did *something* to make him think you were gay."

"You're the one who hugged me in front of him," I countered. "It was a really long hug, too."

"Was not. It was, like, three seconds max, and besides, I hadn't seen you in a week!"

"Oh, please. It was at least ten, and that's no excuse."

"It wasn't ten," she insisted. We fell silent for a moment.

"Was too," I mumbled.

We pulled into my driveway a minute later, and Sarah parked the car, then turned to face me. "Okay. Are we doing this or not?"

"I don't see how we can stop now," I told her, throwing my hands into the air hopelessly. "If we walk into school tomorrow and tell them we made it all up and we're straight, we'll humiliate Jake and they'll hate us for lying. Not to mention it'll seem like we were just making fun of them today."

"Right. So..." she trailed off uncertainly. "We *are* gonna do this? I mean, when you think about it, anyway, there are a lot of pros, and the only con is that people will hate us if they find out, which we're kind of already dealing with anyway. What's the downside to trying it?"

"The bigger the lie, the bigger the fallout," I told her dismally. "But... this is already pretty big. We just told fake stories about realizing we liked girls."

"I could be a lesbian for eight months," Sarah mused, and then grinned at me. "I mean, you're cute."

"I really, *really* hate you right now," I sighed out, and her smile died a little. "This really sucks."

"I know. I'm an idiot. But if things are going badly, we'll just say we're actually bi, plant a few seeds about not being happy together, and break up a little while later, right? Mess taken care of, and we come out mostly unscathed while still keeping everyone happy."

"This still feels dirty," I told her, shaking my head. "And super offensive."

"Then we'll do so much good we can't possibly feel bad," Sarah insisted. "I mean, this club does volunteer work for gay people and all that. We can help. And we're helping by giving them some rep, anyway. We'll be like gay advocates, only secretly straight. And they'll love us."

"We have to lie for eight months. What about our parents?" I realized with a start. "I can't tell them I'm gay when I'm not!'

"Well, mine aren't around all that much anyway, so I have no problems keeping this from them. I guess what you tell yours is up to you."

"They'd tell me to be honest with everyone if I told them the truth. So I have to either lie, or just not mention it and hope it never comes up." I reached up to rub at my temples. "This is crazy."

"People who are in love do crazy things," Sarah sighed out dramatically, raising my hand to her lips and kissing the back of it. I glared at her, unamused. "Oh, c'mon. You're gonna have to get used to it."

"I'm not kissing you," I deadpanned. "Ever."

"Well *there's* something we can agree on."

"Good." I got out of her car with another shake of my head, and she whistled at me as I walked to the front door of my house.

"Lookin' good!"

I stuck my middle finger in the air without turning around, and heard her laughing even as she asked, "Too soon?"

"Bye, Sarah," I sighed out.

She just drove away, still chuckling even as I finished my walk inside. It didn't occur to me until I was in the kitchen with my mom and she was asking me, "So how did your little club meeting go?" that I was monumentally and irreversibly *screwed.*

Chapter Three

Sarah picked me up the next morning, dark circles under her eyes that matched the ones under my own. Her phone went off several times in succession even as I was getting into her car, and I mumbled tiredly, "You too?"

"Yep. My phone's been crazy since yesterday afternoon. Why do teenagers gossip so much?"

"I got no sleep last night," I told her, and leaned back in my seat, closing my eyes as she began to drive.

"Me either. How was your reception? Everyone that texted me figured I was bi, so I guess I'm gonna have to just go with that. Can't pull off full lesbian. Surprise, surprise. Hopefully that'll be enough for Sam."

"I spent three hours texting Dina," I told her, choosing to ignore her Sam comment.

"I wondered why I didn't hear from her," Sarah replied. "Was she cool?"

"Yeah. Really cool, actually. It was kind of nice… other than the fact that, you know, I was completely lying to her the whole time."

"What'd you say?"

"That I'd struggled with my sexuality recently when I realized I had feelings for you, and that now we're in love."

"Awww. You fake love me?"

"I love you in real life, idiot," I mumbled, opening my eyes to roll them at her. "You're just absolutely exhausting to be friends with sometimes. Anyway, who'd you talk to?"

"Everyone," she sighed out. "I think Hannah's a little surprised, but everyone else was strangely… *not*. Which was a little weird because, you know, not actually bi. Then there was Connor, who just begged for a threesome."

"Gross."

"Yeah, I ignored him. But anyway, it made me think that we need a story." She reached over abruptly and took my hand, and I shot her a strange look.

"What are you doing?"

She glanced back at me, grinning. "What? If we're gonna be a couple we have to get used to it."

"We're not a couple." I pulled my hand back. "There's no one watching, so what's the point?"

"I'm a method actress." She grabbed my hand again with another smile, and I glared out of my window, not bothering to fight her on it anymore.

"Just don't get too method," I mumbled.

She laughed at that. "Your general anger at this entire situation is hilarious. I'm not even gonna lie."

"Well, I'm glad at least one of us is amused." I sighed, and then turned to face her. "So what's our story then, method actress?"

"Okay. We already told everyone that we've been together since around the time you and Austin broke up, and that I knew I liked girls early on and you only just figured it out."

"You know... I think you pined away for me for years in secret, hoping one day I'd see you the way you've always seen me." I smirked at her even as she gasped in mock-offense.

"*What*? Why do *I* have to be the piner?"

"Because you got us into this mess and because it only makes sense, since you supposedly knew you liked girls long before I did."

"Fair enough," she agreed half-heartedly. "But you kissed me first."

"No way! No one would buy that," I argued.

She mulled it over for a moment. "Okay, true."

"I told Dina you kissed me first, anyway," I explained. "A couple weeks after I broke up with Austin. And that that was when I realized I liked girls, and we've been dating ever since."

"You're lucky I didn't say anything that contradicts that," she warned me. "We need to do a better job comparing notes."

"Well, this was a *little* on the fly, genius."

"Last question," she said. "Have we had sex?"

"No." I immediately shook my head emphatically, and she gaped at me.

"What? Why not? You don't wanna have sex with me?"

"If we say we've had sex, we'll never hear the end of questions about it, and then we have to answer questions about lesbian sex that we are *obviously* not qualified to answer."

"Oh c'mon, how hard could it be? Besides, that question was mostly a formality; we've *definitely* had sex. If our fake story involves years of pining on my part then there's no way I've been with you for two months and not gotten laid."

"Well, that's charming. That really makes me want to let you be the girl I gave my lesbian virginity to," I deadpanned, letting go of her hand to fold my arms over my chest. "You're not getting into my pants with *that* kind of attitude."

"I'm not getting into your pants at all," she laughed out, grinning widely. "But I'm not gonna tell people that because there's no way I'm that lame. So we're just gonna have to learn about lesbian sex and field the pervy questions we get as well as we can. We can tell the ruder ones to take a hike, and for the rest, we know the basics. Lesbians just do what we do to ourselves except-"

I clapped my hands to my ears before she could finish, and gave her a pointed look even as she started laughing again.

"I don't wanna hear it!" I groaned out.

"Get used to it, Katie. Not only do you have to hear about it, you enjoy doing it."

"I don't know if I can do this." I sighed and looked out my window again as we pulled into our school parking lot.

"You better pull yourself together," Sarah replied, her expression serious now. "It's show time."

I'd say I felt like an ant under a magnifying class that first day, but that doesn't do it justice. There were eyes *everywhere*. And the only thing that felt strong about me in that moment, as Sarah and I walked down the hallway together, was her hand's numbing grip on mine. I wondered, then, if she liked the attention, since most of it seemed to come from guys.

I, personally, wanted to crawl into a cave somewhere and never come out. The stares came with whispers, and I was almost thankful I couldn't really catch anything anyone was saying. I was scared it was bad, and I was also scared it was good.

We reached my locker and Sarah let go of my hand. The students nearest us tried to act like they weren't stealing glances at us, but it was obvious they were, and I gave Sarah the subtlest of head-shakes as we stood together. As confident as she'd seemed beside me as we'd walked, I could see she looked nervous now, too.

"That was terrible," I murmured, and to my surprise, she nodded her agreement and swallowed hard, whispering her response.

"Being gay is definitely already harder than I thought it'd be. But we signed up for it."

I shook my head again. "You did."

She looked down and away from me, and I gathered my stuff out of my locker quickly, eager to just get to class. As I closed my locker, I heard Sarah say, "Hey."

When I turned around, Colton, the boy from one of our classes, was standing in front of Sarah, a grin on his face. "Hey, Sarah. Katie. How are you guys?"

Sarah and I exchanged looks, and I forced a smile, answering for us. "Same as ever. How are you?"

"Good. I'm really great." His grin returned as soon as he finished speaking, and he looked back and forth between us, like he was waiting for something. It was uncomfortable.

"Cool," Sarah finally replied, breaking the silence. "Well, we have to get to class now."

"That's fine." He shook his head and stepped aside. "Just keep doing what you're doing. It's cool. I know *I* approve."

"Thanks," I said shortly, and quickly pulled Sarah away and down the hall, her giggling all the while.

"Oh my God, he's so weird," she murmured to me.

Except we quickly realized that he wasn't.

Colton was the first of many, *many* guys that day who felt the need to gawk at us, tell us we were hot, announce their approval, or all three. We got questions about threesomes, questions about what we did in bed – all of which were completely invasive and inappropriate and absolutely qualified as "rude" – and questions about which one of us was the man in our relationship. We were whistled at, catcalled at, stared at, and shouted after, and I got called a "dyke" twice in casual conversation. That all happened over the course of seven hours, but even by lunch that day, I felt like crying.

I know it showed on my face as I sat down, because Dina took one look at me and reached across the table to take my hands into hers. "You okay, Katie? I know it must be rough."

"I feel like I showed up to school naked or something," I marveled. "I say I'm dating a girl and suddenly all everyone cares about is my sex life. Like, can't I just take a punch and be done with it?"

As if to prove my point, Connor arrived at our table and took a seat, smirking at me. "Hey, Katie. Heard about you and Sarah... so what's that like and where do I buy tickets?"

"Leave her alone, Connor," Josephine snapped at him even as Dina opened her mouth to do the same. Graham and Bonnie were silent beside us, but I saw Graham roll his eyes in Connor's direction, and that made me feel a little better. At least most of my friends were going to be cool about this.

I let out a deep breath and started to pick at my food, trying to keep myself grounded. None of this was real. I wasn't actually gay. And if I wanted to make this go away, I could. I'd just have to tell Sarah to start the breakup plan as soon as possible.

She joined our table soon with Hannah at her side, completing our usual group of eight. "Hey guys. We all good?"

"Of course. We love you and Katie." Dina offered her a smile and then tilted her head in my direction. "I hear you guys have been having a tough day, huh?"

"Yeah. Lots of asshole guys, mostly," said Sarah. "I'd be fine with it if they weren't all so graphic, seriously. Like, I'm the bi one and I still really don't wanna know exactly what you'd do to me and my girlfriend if you got us alone, so I can't imagine what it's like for Katie to have to hear it all day."

"It'll die down, I'm sure. You guys are new and shiny today," Josephine pointed out. "Everyone's gotta get their two cents in."

As Sarah nodded beside me, I couldn't help but inwardly marvel at her. She'd slipped into her new role so effortlessly, and here I was, already trying to hit the abort button.

I felt a tap on my shoulder and my heart sank into my stomach. I knew what was coming: more comments from people I hardly knew.

I turned in my seat and it was an understatement to say that I was pleasantly surprised to see Jake. I practically threw myself into his arms, still seated, and he laughed sympathetically, leaning down to hug me back. "Hard day?"

"You're in this lunch period?" I asked him, pulling away, and he nodded, pointing to a table across the cafeteria. I could see Hattie, Jessa, and a few other familiar faces from LAMBDA sitting there. Jessa, the girl who hadn't seemed to believe Sarah and I's story yesterday, was now watching Jake and me with interest. I wondered briefly if she was still suspicious of us.

"Yeah," Jake said. "Just thought I'd come and say hi, and let you know that if you need any advice, we're here. We all remember our first days, too. The second day is *so* much easier. I mean, I remember after the first I thought I'd made this massive mistake, and I wanted so badly to just go back to being closeted. But obviously I couldn't do that, so." He shrugged. "Anyway, if either of you need anything, here's my number." He handed me a slip of paper, and I nodded my thanks. "I'll be around," he finished, and left.

When I turned back around, everyone else was watching me curiously.

"Who was that?" Connor asked, eyeing Jake as he walked back to his own table.

"Our gay guru," Sarah explained. "He convinced us to come out. His name's Jake. He's president of the gay club at our school."

"Our school has a gay club?" Hannah asked, amused. "Why haven't I heard of it?"

"Maybe because you're not gay?" Sarah proposed with a smirk. "It's very exclusive. You have to be the gayest of the gay to get in."

"And yet they let you in anyway," Hannah quipped. "Boy-crazy Sarah. If you can get in, I'll bet anyone can."

"Hey, there's only one person I'm crazy about anymore, and I have verifiable proof that she is not a boy. I'm gay enough."

I rolled my eyes at the two of them, feeling a flush crawl up my cheeks as Hannah laughed, and then busied myself by putting Jake's number into my phone. I stared down at his name for a moment, then let out a small sigh and put my phone back into my purse.

I couldn't call off this thing with Sarah, I knew. At least not this early. Not when Jake and Hattie and Jessa and Violet and all of the other LAMBDA kids hadn't been able to do the same. It felt wrong to even consider it.

Our lunch group moved on after that to some of our more usual topics, and we all fell into easier, casual conversation. Dina and Josephine talked about the cute guy in their Spanish class, and Graham asked Sarah if she'd help him study for a test he had next week. Not much was different, if anything at all, and that was the best I could've ever hoped for, so I was happy to know I'd chosen my friends well. I mean, Connor was always going to be kind of a jerk, because that was how Connor was, but he was tame compared to the comments I now knew I'd be getting in the future.

Meanwhile, Sarah, for her part, was kind of a natural at being my girlfriend. Or maybe just at being *a* girlfriend. I'd only ever dated Austin, and

61

we had a lot of... *unique* coupley quirks that basically meant I didn't have much experience with acting like a girl who'd fallen head over heels for someone and couldn't keep her hands off of them. Sarah, however, had dated plenty of boys, and knew how it was done.

But there were some things I knew she hadn't had experience with, because they were things she wouldn't have done with boys. She tucked my hair behind my ear when it got in my face while I was eating lunch, and later, she carried a book for me between two of our classes. It was actually a little funny, but only because Sarah made it funny by making it really obvious that she knew she was being a good girlfriend. As we walked back to her car together after school, hand in hand, she whispered, "If we were actually dating, you'd so be repaying me in sexual favors tonight."

I started laughing, hard, and it was like most of the stress from that day just melted right off of me. She grinned back, lighting up at what seemed to be just the sight of a smile from me after I'd had such a rough day, and then she started the car and we began the drive to her house, where we planned to spend the rest of the afternoon learning how to make ourselves a convincing gay couple.

And I didn't realize it then, as Sarah and I left the parking lot and sped down the road in her little four-door, but I think that by the end of that very first school day I'd already fallen a little bit in love with her.

Chapter Four

Sarah's bedroom was, frankly, massive. Posters covered the majority of the wall space and she had a king-sized bed that took up a quarter of the room. The other three-fourths of it housed a desk where she kept her laptop, a bookshelf on which rested all of her favorite books, her dresser, and a flat-screen television I was more than a little jealous of.

She also had a lot of room to sprawl out on her floor between the TV and the bed, so that was what I did, clicking through television channels as Sarah sat beside me with her laptop resting in her lap. "So it looks like we have a lot of shows to get through," she told me. "I can cover books, since I'm the bigger reader between the two of us, but that means you have to handle music."

"There's gay music?" I asked.

"Duh. Haven't you heard of Madonna?" She did some more clicking, and then corrected, "Wait, that's gay men. We need to listen to Tegan and Sara, Ani Difranco, and K.D. Lang. Or at least know a couple big songs from each."

"What about television?" I asked. "Maybe we can get away with not watching it as long as we get the main plots memorized."

"Well, the big one is *The L Word*," Sarah explained. "It's about a group of lesbians from, like, California. Then they all hook up with people. Like *Sex and the City* but gay." She clicked around for a few more seconds. "*Glee* and *Pretty Little Liars* are on here too; we've seen those so we're good. But I haven't heard of any of these movies, wow."

"Let me see." I leaned over her shoulder to look at a list she'd pulled up. None of them rang a bell, with the exception of one. "Wait. How is *Bend It like Beckham* a gay movie?"

"Maybe we missed something when we watched it the first time." Sarah looked like she was trying not to laugh. "Okay, anyway, we're gonna have to study if we want to pull this off. Didn't you get the *tiniest* feeling that that Jessa girl didn't buy any of it yesterday?" She grinned as she asked the question.

"Yeah," I sighed out. "Just slightly."

"So if we can learn a little bit about each of these movies, she'll think we took the time to watch them all, which makes us way more convincing. And I say we pick one to watch tonight, and then you go home and watch the pilot episode of *The L Word* while I try to find an online pdf of a popular young adult lesbian novel. Tomorrow morning, we finish trading notes, and mission accomplished, we are officially knowledgeable about lesbian culture."

"Why am I totally unsurprised that you're treating this like a school project you need to ace?" I sighed out. "Do you really think it's worth doing so much work? I mean, obviously we want to put some sort of effort in, but say we don't necessarily go the extra mile and then one girl doesn't buy it. Does it really matter as long as everyone else does?"

"That one girl could cause a lot of problems if she gets snoopy," Sarah pointed out. "And besides, you're the one who wanted us to do something good here. If we learn about lesbians, we'll come to understand more about them, and then we'll be more open-minded in the future."

"They're not aliens, Sarah," I mumbled, going back to channel-surfing. "They just date girls instead of guys. Not that hard to understand."

"I know that. Look, it just can't hurt to be prepared. You know how I am."

"Yeah, alright. Fine," I gave in. There was no use arguing with her when she was on a mission to learn something. "Just tell me what to do."

We spent the next two hours memorizing character names and plotlines and movie titles and endings, and it wasn't fun. Sarah did a better job than me, which wasn't surprising, but I had to admit I was a little impressed with her even though I hated having to do all of the memorization in the first place. Yes, she'd made the blunder that'd gotten us to where we were now, but she seemed to realize the ramifications of her actions and was now genuinely trying to make the best of it.

She sent me home with a link to the pilot episode of that show she wanted me to watch, and once I'd gotten through dinner with my parents – which had become much more stressful over the past couple of days now that I was keeping a massive secret from them – I headed to my bedroom and forced myself to start the show. It was like Sarah'd described: six women in California were gay and did gay things and had gay drama. But it kind of sucked me in, honestly. By the end of the first episode I considered watching the second, but then I realized I was about to get sucked into a show explicitly for and about and probably *by* lesbians, and I couldn't get past that mental block.

My phone went off on my nightstand just as I was setting my laptop aside. I had one new text message from an unknown number. It said: *"So here is something random, and u don't know me. U should get ur shit together and go out with me."*

I stared as I tried to make sense of the less-than-intelligent string of words, and when they finally sank in, my grip tightened on the phone and I resisted the urge to reply. Instead, I scrolled down my contact list until I came to Jake's number, and then debated only for a moment before I pressed the button to call him.

He sounded a little sleepy when he picked up. "Hello?"

"Hey, Jake. It's Katie." I laid back on my bed and stared up at my bedroom ceiling as I asked him, "Did I wake you up?"

"It's fine; I was just taking a nap. Is everything okay?"

"Not so much." I sighed and closed my eyes. "Some idiot got my cell number, so I'm getting harassed from the safety of my own bedroom now, which is lovely."

"I'm sorry, Katie," said Jake. "All I can say is that you have to focus on the good. Your friends all still love you, right? A lot of people that come out can't say that."

"But what am I supposed to do about everyone else? I have to spend every day with people staring and making comments and sending stupid anonymous texts to me about how I need to get my shit together and go out with a guy? How do you deal with it?"

"You need to start blocking numbers, honey," he told me. "That's the only thing you can do about the texts. For the people at school... you can only do what the rest of us do: Learn to be snarky, get a thick skin, and hope it gets better. People react to girls and guys differently though when we come out. Someone like Jessa could probably give you better advice than me."

"I don't think she likes me," I admitted. "She was a little cold at the first meeting."

"She just takes some time to warm up to new people," he said. "Give her until next Tuesday, when we all meet up again. And look, Katie, try to remember that you're really lucky. A lot of us don't have someone by our side when we come out. You have Sarah. Just being there for each other is gonna help both of you out a lot. I mean, imagine if you were alone in all of this."

"Yeah," I told him faintly, thinking that even after just one day of faking being gay *and* of having Sarah by my side throughout it all, it was easy to see why so many other gay kids wound up clinically depressed. Sarah had thought it'd be easy to be a lesbian, and while I'd had the presence of mind to know this wouldn't be easy, I'd had no idea it'd be this hard. "I'll see you tomorrow, Jake." I said. "Bye."

"Bye, Katie."

I didn't see him the next day, and that turned out to be one of many of in a string of disappointments I experienced that day. It started with small stuff: Annie, the girl I sometimes exchanged hellos or waves with in the hallway when we'd pass each other on our way to class, decided that our new tradition was that *I'd* wave and *she'd* look at her feet and ignore me. So that was cool.

I pretty much forgot about that, though, when I ran into Austin. We nearly crashed head-on in the hallway, looked up, saw each other, and then did everything we could to hastily side-step each other and move on. As he walked away, I heard some guy shout something to him that I couldn't quite make out. I spent my next class period wondering if Sarah and I's lie had had negative consequences for Austin somehow, and I walked around with a heavy heart for the rest of the day.

Sarah wasn't much help, and the reason for that was obvious: Sam Heath spoke to her. It was while we were at her locker together, and it wasn't much: just a sly "cute" as he eyed the two of us up and down while on his way to class, but I thought Sarah might burst out into song at any moment, and I had to elbow her in the side to remind her she was supposed to be into *me* and not Sam. It wasn't until Sarah'd already gone off to her next class that I saw Jessa glance at me from just a few lockers down, and realized that if she'd seen that entire exchange, we were probably screwed.

And as if that wasn't nerve-wracking enough, I also had a pop quiz.

It all wasn't as bad as yesterday had been, but it wasn't great, either, and I still left school feeling terrible. Sarah and I walked out to her car together; she planned to drive me home today so we could finally share what we'd learned last night. Before we could get into her car, however, the last person I expected to see trying to talk to me jogged over to us.

Austin's hands were shoved into his pockets and his lanky form was hunched over just slightly, like he was trying to humble himself. His eyes darted back and forth between us as he cleared his throat uncomfortably, and I nearly jumped when I felt Sarah's arm snake possessively around my waist.

"What do you want, Austin?" she asked him, and I could practically sense her eyes narrowing at my side. I wondered how hilarious she was finding this, inwardly.

"Uh... can I talk to you, Katie?" he asked, his voice quiet. "I promise it'll be quick."

"It's fine," I said, both to him and to Sarah, and he nodded his thanks, turning and walking away. I followed, and when we were out of Sarah's earshot, he paused and faced me, letting out a sigh and squeezing his eyes shut.

"Okay." He looked at me. "The whole school's saying you and Sarah are..."

"Yeah," I interrupted swiftly, biting my lip. "I know."

"So that... back there, she was-" He cut himself off and glanced behind me, where Sarah stood, probably watching us. "I just wanted to know if that... if that was why we... why you ended things with us." His eyes found his feet. "Everyone's saying I turned you gay."

I watched him carefully for a moment. The heavy feeling in my chest intensified, and I didn't know what to tell him. Which was better: To lie and tell him I'd left him for Sarah, or to be honest and say I'd left him because I just didn't want to be with him? I wasn't even sure being left for a girl was preferable to being left for no one at all.

"You didn't turn me gay, Austin," I said at last. "People either are gay or they aren't. Anyone who tries to tell you you ruined guys for me is full of crap."

That answer didn't seem to satisfy him. "Look, all I'm saying is that you broke up with me without any explanation. I'm trying to get one now."

"Why now?" I asked him. "I wanted to talk to you right after it happened, but you ignored me."

"Yeah, I was a little pissed," he shot back. "Can you blame me? You were the girl of my dreams and you dumped me."

I sighed, trying to keep calm. "I get that. I do. But I still wanted to be friends. I still want to *now.*"

"Well, I don't know if I'm ready for that," he said. "But it might help to know that at least you were just gay and I didn't do anything wrong. You started dating Sarah right after we broke up, right? Did you leave me for her?"

He was looking at me knowingly now, and I swallowed hard. "No."

He shook his head. "That's bullshit, Katie. C'mon."

"I didn't," I insisted. "That happened after. All of it."

"And you expect me to believe our breakup was totally about the two of us even though you switched teams and started dating your best friend within a few weeks? We were together for a *year.*"

"Look, I broke up with you because I never had feelings for you, okay?" I burst, and it was like the floodgates in my chest had been opened, and everything I'd held back to spare his feelings when we'd broken up came pouring out now. "You were my first everything, and I know that that's special and all, but I just didn't feel the way about you that

I could tell you felt about me. You were a nice guy, and I felt pressured to start dating because all of my friends were doing it. I mean, I cared about you, but it wasn't-"

"Like it is with her," he cut me off. His eyes were looking past me again, at Sarah. "I get it. So you really always were gay." He turned away, adding a quick, "See you," and I had to bite my tongue to stop myself from correcting him as he walked away; to stop myself from pointing out that just because I didn't like *him* didn't mean I didn't like boys. But that would've blown my cover, and so I let him walk away, and then rejoined Sarah by her car, where she was leaning against it, idly examining her fingernails.

"What'd he want?" she asked.

"Validation," I told her shortly, and she wisely didn't ask any more questions.

Despite my conversation with Austin, Sarah and I had an amusing drive home. As it turned out, she'd been worse than me; I'd feared she'd tease me when I revealed that *The L Word* was actually mildly addicting, but in reality I'd showed restraint where she had not. The young adult novel she'd found had taken four hours to read, and so that's what Sarah had done from about six to ten o'clock last night.

"And how was the ending? Satisfying?" I asked her, grinning from ear to ear.

"Shut up. It was okay. They didn't end up together though, which was total bullshit."

"Why not? It seems pointless otherwise."

"Well, one of the chicks was just experimenting, so she went back to guys and the other one realized she was actually into girls. The story was more about the second girl, I think. Anyway, how was *The L Word*?"

"Uh, sexual." I shrugged.

"Sounds like my kind of show," she joked. "So how many episodes did you watch?"

"Just the one I was supposed to." I shot her a sly smile. "Why, did you expect me to have spent, say... *four hours* on it?"

"Shut up!" she repeated, but she was hiding a smile. "It was a good book. What happened on the show, seriously?"

"Um... I don't know. Girls hooked up, there was this writer girl with a boyfriend – Jenny – but you can tell she's gonna realize she's gay."

"So what I'm gathering from this is that you should know how to have lesbian sex now."

"Oh, I'm an expert." I rolled my eyes at her as she chuckled. "I'll teach you all about it."

"I'm sure you will." She winked as we pulled into my driveway, and I rolled my eyes again as I got out of the car.

"Thanks for the ride."

"Anything for my girlfriend." She grinned. "Especially since we're *cute* together!"

"The obsession never stops," I deadpanned, waving goodbye to her.

"Never!" she called back as she drove away.

I dodged dinner this time and spent the rest of the night in my room alone, absorbing and reevaluating everything I'd been through in the past few days.

I was torn on what to do about Sarah and I's little ruse. She'd hate the idea of calling it off now, I knew, given that she'd gotten one more word than usual out of Sam, but I didn't feel obligated to her, honestly. I felt obligated to Jake and to the other LAMBDA members... and I have to admit I was a little afraid of how much worse I'd be treated for *faking* lesbianism, given how awful it was to actually *be* a lesbian.

I could picture the insults now, from the shallow ones to the ones that attacked the very core of who we were: that we'd do anything for attention; that we'd manipulated and used a minority group for our own gain. Maybe we really were already in too deep to back out now.

But at least tomorrow was Friday, and all I had to do was get through seven more hours of school and then I'd be able to take the weekend to have some quiet time to myself.

I got on my laptop eventually, and hadn't been online for more than a half-hour before a window popped up telling me that Sarah was requesting a video chat. Confused, I accepted, and a second later her face was on my laptop screen.

"You are not gonna believe this bullshit," she fumed, trying to show me something on her phone. I squinted, the blurry video quality making it hard to see.

Finally, the picture cleared and I could barely make out the words of a text message. I read aloud, "Hey, I hear bi chicks are freakier in bed. Come sit on my-" I made a disgusted face and stopped reading, and Sarah pulled her phone away, looking embarrassed.

"Sorry, wrong text."

"Wait, who sent that?" I asked her.

"Unknown number. Whatever," she shrugged it off, and if I hadn't known her as well as I did, I might've genuinely believed she was unaffected. "*This* is the one I meant to show you."

"Wait, I'm getting them, too. I figured you'd be cut some slack because you're not saying you're a lesbian, though."

"Yeah, well, apparently the bisexuals don't have it all that great, either." She sounded impatient. "Look, that's nothing compared to this."

I forced myself to drop the subject for the time being, and focused on the new message she was holding up to the screen. It was another from an unknown number, but the text cleared up who'd sent it right from the beginning. "This is Jessa. I saw you in the hallway and I know what you two are up to, and it's really shitty of you to use actual gay people like this. I'll give you until the meeting on Tuesday to come clean or else I'm telling everyone. I'm serious." My eyes widened. "Uh, that's not good."

"Can you believe she'd send me that?" Sarah yanked the phone back, infuriated all over again.

I shifted uncomfortably, already thinking ahead. God, people were going to absolutely loathe us. But a part of me was glad that the lying would be short-lived. I don't think I could've pulled off an entire eight months, so it was all kind of bound to come crashing down eventually. I just hoped we wouldn't lose our friends from lunch. "Well..." I hesitated. "I mean, yeah. She's right."

"That doesn't mean she gets to call me out on it! Doesn't she know who we are?"

I rested my chin in my hands and let out a sigh. "Yeah, considering everyone else does, I'd imagine so."

"How are you being so chill about this? Like, if we don't do something drastic our cover is blown."

"Something drastic? It kind of seems like it's blown regardless. There isn't anything we can do except to apologize and hope Jake and everyone else doesn't hate us, and then do what we can to make amends if they do."

She shook her head. "No way. C'mon, we can't only last *two days*, Katie. We just need to work a little harder."

"You always do this," I sighed out. "Sometimes you can stockpile every resource you have and it just isn't enough, Sarah. We did the homework and we did a decent enough acting job, but *you* were the one who gave it away by obsessing over Sam. You know that's what she saw, right?"

Sarah groaned, and her head fell forward into her hands. "We're seriously gonna go down like this, though?"

I watched her for a moment, and swallowed hard. "I mean, you got us into this, so if either of us has the right to be mad or disappointed or upset, it's me."

She raised her head, and I expected a snippy retort or a glare from her. Instead, she looked inspired. "Wait. I got us into this, right?"

"I just said that," I told her, exasperated now.

"And you had no choice in the matter."

"It's nice to hear you admit that," I deadpanned. "Yes, I had no choice and now my reputation is gonna go down in a blaze of not-glory."

"Maybe not."

"Sarah, she *knows.* Give it up. We're surrounded; just put your hands in the air and surrender." I could tell from the way she was tapping her chin with her finger that I was about to be entirely ignored. "Sarah," I tried again anyway, "you're smart. If a cop caught you in the middle of committing a crime, would you really try to convince them you hadn't done it?"

"...No..." she answered vaguely.

"No," I echoed. "You'd plead guilty and hope for a laxer sentence."

She mulled that over for a moment, and then smirked at me. "But it's like you said... how much of a difference can one girl make?"

"Meaning?"

"Meaning Jessa isn't the cop. She's the prosecutor, and that means we've just gotta convince that twelve-member LAMBDA jury."

Chapter Five

Mom insisted on spending Saturday having a "girls' day" while Dad went out for lunch with a couple of guys he'd known back in college who were visiting from Atlanta. She gave me the option to invite Sarah along, but I decided against it.

Sarah was on this self-indulgent "I'm gonna use my superior knowledge to get us out of this" kick and also wouldn't tell me anything about what her plan was, so I'd mostly spent Friday just going through the motions with her. We visited our lockers together, walked to class together, and generally did everything we'd done for the past several years as friends together, only with bonus hand-holding, and I tried hard not to notice Jessa

81

throughout the day, who seemed to be watching us everywhere we went.

Sarah, to her credit, ignored not only Jessa but also Sam – even when he blatantly stared at us and tried to get her attention at one point –, but that was the only indication I got that she had some sort of plan she was implementing. Knowing her, she probably just planned to tone down her heterosexuality for a few days and then try to talk her way out of the mess she'd made at the LAMBDA meeting next Tuesday. I wasn't sure whether I wanted her to succeed or not anymore, honestly.

My mom and I went to go see a movie, but before that, we grabbed lunch at this little bistro a short walk away from the theater.

"So you've been quiet this week," she observed as we ate. "Is everything okay?"

"Fine," I said. "Just always hate the first week back after a break. No more free time."

"Well, if it's more free time you're after, you don't necessarily have to go to that club Sarah talked you into joining," Mom pointed out. "What was it again? Some kind of volunteer club?"

"Yeah, um..." I took a bite and chewed slowly to give myself some time to think. "It's animal-based. You know I've always loved dogs, so."

"Oh, are they volunteering at shelters?" she asked. I nodded. "That's nice. But even so, if it's making you exhausted, it's not worth it. Your grades are good enough that you don't need any extracurriculars to get you into Creswell."

She was right. My college application, which I'd be sending out any week now, was only going to a few local schools, the best of which was Creswell State University. I was a shoe-in. Not like Sarah, who was shooting for Emory and needed all the help she could get.

"I'm fine, Mom," I insisted. "Don't worry about me."

"Well, that's a tall order from my only child," she joked. "If I don't worry about you, what am I supposed to worry about?"

"I don't know." I hid a smile. "Menopause?"

"Katie! I am not that old," she said, and reached across the table to slap playfully at my arm.

"Right, I forgot. You're a young, hip Mom. Even hipper than Amy Poehler was in *Mean Girls*."

"Exactly."

I raised my head to grin at her. "That was a test. No one says 'hip' anymore."

"Well if I can't be hip, at least I'm groovy," she replied, and then smiled when I laughed through a mouthful of food.

"Please don't repeat that around my friends."

"Only around Sarah," she promised. "She accepts me and all I have to do in return is talk her into eating my dinners every now and then." I felt my smile die slightly, and Mom, being Mom, immediately caught on and went into mothering mode. "I knew it; you two are fighting, aren't you?"

"Mom," I whined, drawing the word out, "Sarah and I are not fighting, okay? Everything's seriously fine. I promise."

"Then why haven't I seen her since Monday? Did you two fight that day you went over to her house?"

"No," I said. "We're fine."

"If you use the word 'fine' one more time I'll call her myself," Mom joked. "Honey, friends fight all the time. You two have had your fair share, from what I can recall. It always works itself out."

"We're not fighting!" I insisted. "Can you please just drop it?"

I didn't realize how loud I'd been until I caught several nearby diners shooting glances at us. Mom set down her silverware with a sigh, speaking quietly. "Katie, honey, you need to keep your voice down."

I chewed on my bottom lip, embarrassed. "I'm sorry. I've just had a rough week. That's all. Sarah and I are fine... we're *okay*. It's just me. I've been..." I hesitated, and then admitted, "I've been getting teased again."

Mom's face fell immediately, but there was an understanding in her expression that relieved me. Provided I could avoid giving her any details, this was a safe, believable, and semi-truthful route to take. "Oh, honey. About what?"

"Just stuff," I mumbled. "I don't wanna talk about it."

"Certainly not about your weight? You know you're a beautiful girl, don't you? You're perfectly healthy."

"Yeah, I know," I told her half-heartedly. "I'm not gonna stop eating again. People... just suck sometimes, is all."

"Does Sarah stick up for you?" Mom asked.

"That's not her job," I deflected. "It wasn't her job in middle school and it's not now."

"But in middle school she did it anyway," Mom reminded me.

"Well, she has her own stuff to worry about now," I said.

"Oh, I see," she said. "So like that boy and your new club."

"I guess." I nudged at the food on my plate with my fork. "It's nothing I can't handle. Anyway, aren't we gonna be late for the movie?"

"Don't change the subject," she chided me, but motioned for our waiter to bring the check nonetheless. "You're a strong girl, Katie. You've been through a lot more than most girls your age. Sarah or no Sarah, you can handle bullies. I'd just sleep easier at night knowing you have someone on your side."

"I do. Believe me, Sarah may be busy, but she and I are definitely in this one together."

"Well, good. I'm glad you have her. That girl's always had a unique way with words; that's for sure."

"I come here today, accused."

I pressed my lips together and tried to follow my instructions from Sarah as best as I could, but given that she'd left me completely in the dark from Thursday night through... well, five minutes before our LAMBDA meeting, and given that my only instructions were to "just look victimized" because she's "got this", I was a little lost and more than a little disheartened by her opening statement. Regardless of how many years she'd spent on our middle school debate team, this seemed like the wrong way to approach our dilemma, to say the least.

Nearly everyone else in the room, including Jake *and* Jessa, looked just as startled by Sarah's statement as I felt. Five minutes into our LAMBDA meeting, she'd asked that she be given the floor in the center of our little circle in order to make an announcement, and now here we were, staring at her while she spoke, confident and indignant.

As I watched, one eyebrow raised, she pointed an accusing finger at Jessa, who responded with an expression that probably looked pretty similar to my own. "Jessa here doesn't seem to believe that Katie and I are a real couple."

Now it was Jessa's turn to look indignant. She rose from her seat. "Because you-!"

"Hey!" Sarah cut her off. "It's my turn to talk. If you want the floor, you can have it when I'm done." As Jessa let out a disbelieving laugh and took a seat with a shake of her head, Sarah addressed the rest of the group. "Look, I've known Katie for practically my whole life. A lot of you guys have, too. Have you ever known her to throw herself at boys? No, right? Because she's gay."

I tried hard to keep a straight face as she pressed on. There was no way this was going to work. Sarah had school smarts, but she put her foot in her mouth *way* too much for this to go smoothly. She'd been a terrible debater in middle school, honestly, but I'm not sure anyone ever had the heart to tell her.

"And I'll admit I have a bad reputation," she continued, "but I don't think it's right to just assume I'm faking a relationship with my best friend just because I like boys, too. Bisexuals can settle down, you know."

"She has a point, Jessa," Hattie chimed in, looking mildly offended. "*I'm* bisexual, and I've mostly dated girls. Sarah might prefer guys but she can still commit to Katie, and I think it's kind of offensive to imply that she's faking a relationship with a girl just because she's not a lesbian."

"They're *both* faking it," Jessa insisted. "I'm sure they're both straight. At the very, *very* least, Sarah is. She's just doing this to rile up some guy she's trying to sleep with; I've seen her fawning all over him."

"It's called *flirting*, Jessa. It doesn't always mean I'm interested. Maybe if you knew how to do it you'd have a girlfriend, too."

"Alright, guys, c'mon," Jake cut in hastily as Jessa began to get to her feet again. "Look, this is where we come for *support*. It's supposed to be a safe haven to talk about how we feel. Sarah and Katie have been through a lot this week and I think we should cut them some slack."

"Seriously," Sarah echoed, folding her arms across her chest and shooting Jessa a smug look. "There are some real issues we could actually be talking about here, so how about you drop this and move on?"

Jessa, surprisingly, looked just as smug. "Fine, Sarah. I will."

"Good."

"Just do one thing for me real quick, though: Kiss your girlfriend."

Sarah froze in place, and my head swiveled so fast I almost pulled a muscle in my neck.

Thankfully, Sarah recovered quickly. "Um, no. Do I look like your own personal porno?"

"I didn't say you have to make out," Jessa shot back. "It's just a quick kiss. That's no big deal if you've been dating for months and into each other for longer, right? I mean, if you're really *so* in love..."

I tried my best to help her out there, jumping in quickly with a hasty, "Jake."

He came to our rescue. "Jessa, c'mon. They're a couple. Let's move on."

"If they're a couple why won't they kiss?" she asked the group, and I saw a few people exchange thoughtful looks, as though she had somewhat of a point. The unpleasant nervousness that'd been building in my stomach all day began to swell and creep up into my chest.

"Maybe I'm not into PDA," Sarah insisted, but the excuse was flimsy, and Jessa countered it easily.

"Sarah Cooper, not into PDA. Uh huh. That's real convincing."

"Uh, I'm kissing someone in front of thirteen people here, too, you know," I cut in weakly. "I don't like PDA."

"Blah blah blah, all I'm hearing right now is that both of you are making up excuses not to kiss each other. What does that tell us?"

"Sarah. Katie," Hattie said abruptly, drawing both of our gazes to her. "Look, just shut her up. She's just jealous."

"Yeah, I'm just jealous," Jessa echoed, smirking at us. "So go ahead and prove me wrong, ladies."

Sarah and I exchanged looks as she stood in the center of the group and I remained seated. In three seconds, we had a mental conversation that went a little like this:

Her: "???"

Me: "No. No way."

Her: "Are you sure? C'mon! We can't let her win this."

Me: "Sarah, no."

Her: "Yes?"

Me: "No!"

Her: "Oh, just suck it up."

And then, aloud, she sighed heavily and announced, "Okay, this is stupid," stalked over to me even as I gave her the most subtly withering look I could muster, heaved me to my feet by my hand, then gave me a brief look that said: "you better act like you're enjoying this" before pressing her lips to mine.

And I blanked. My hands, completely of their own volition, found their way to her hips and rested against them, and at some point my eyes must have fluttered shut, because right around the time her lips started moving against mine I realized I couldn't see anything.

Her own hands were surprisingly gentle on my cheeks as they cupped my face, and she was kind of an amazing kisser. Her lips were soft and I could taste her favorite lipgloss on them, and for a brief moment, sometime before I remembered where exactly we were, I had the briefest of thoughts: "So *this* is kissing a girl. Huh."

When I first started kissing her back, which took a few seconds, I kissed her like she was Austin. Like she was someone I cared about and wanted to have romantic feelings for, but just couldn't quite get there with. Because that was what she was. It would've been much easier to be a real couple in that moment, surrounded by people who would then have loved us for who we actually were and not for who they thought we were. And it was kind of nice, kissing her like I kissed Austin, because kissing Austin was always kind of nice. Kind of *okay*.

But then it hit me, *really* hit me that she wasn't Austin, that she was my best friend Sarah, and it was like we'd been moving in silent slow motion and now someone had hit the "play" button.

All of my senses were suddenly on hyperdrive.

My lips stuttered against hers and I felt her breath, hot and heavy against my chin as we lost our kiss for a moment, and then her lips caught my bottom lip and I was kissing her like she was Sarah this time, like she was my first kiss with a girl and like there was a nervous ball of tension in my stomach and throughout my chest and like it was both our first kiss and our last. My heart thudded hard, stopped, and then thudded harder, my stomach twisted in a way that was strangely pleasant and entirely terrifying, and then every muscle in my body weakened because her tongue flicked against my lip.

She pulled away first, and her eyes opened right when mine did, dark and blue and wow, *really* dark. The look in them kept my heart racing even as I registered that I was a little out of breath. *Noticeably* out of breath.

Right on cue, a throat cleared and we both followed the noise to Jake, who, to put it lighter than I've ever put anything before in my life, looked *slightly* amused. Beside him, Hattie was pretending to fan herself, and on the other side of the room, even Jessa looked a little bit befuddled.

"So," Jake finally broke the silence, trying hard not to laugh, "I think that settles that. Henry, you had something you wanted to tell us today, didn't you?"

I was suddenly aware that my hands were still on Sarah's hips, and I released them hastily as Jessa grudgingly took a seat and Henry began to tell us all about how he'd come out to his parents over the weekend and they'd reacted well. "Sorry," I mumbled to Sarah as we sat down, embarrassed that my hands had lingered on her sides.

She sounded a little distracted as she replied, "No, it's okay," and while Henry spoke, I saw her lean forward to place an elbow on her crossed legs and rest her chin in her hand. Her fingers traced her lips at least once when she thought I wasn't looking, and my insides twisted again in that way I wasn't used to them twisting.

"Katie," Jake said some few minutes later, and I nearly jumped as I swiveled around to look at him.

"Hmm? Yeah?"

"You and I talked a little about how you've had a hard time dealing with being newly out. I wondered if you wanted to share any of that here."

"Oh, have you guys really had it that bad?" Hattie jumped in before I could reply, sounding genuinely interested. "I thought you were friends with the people who normally do the harassing. No offense or anything."

"We can't be friends with everyone," Sarah told her dully, her chin still in her hand. "Besides, some of it's anonymous."

"Oh, the texts?" Violet asked, speaking for the first time today. "I got them too. Sometimes I still do."

Hattie nodded her agreement. "When guys come out as gay or bi, other guys like to use slurs and physical violence against them. But when girls come out, we get slurs, occasional physical violence, *and* sexual harassment."

"Right?" Sarah chimed in again, straightening up suddenly and gaining some enthusiasm. "Do you have any idea how many threesome requests I've gotten?"

"It's even worse because we're bi," Hattie agreed. "But they'll ask any girl who isn't straight, honestly."

"When I came out," Jessa announced abruptly, and everyone looked to her, surprised she was joining the conversation after Sarah and I had, frankly, given her quite the smackdown just minutes ago.

She cleared her throat and looked straight at us as she continued, "I had a couple guys come up to me after school and corner me in the parking lot, insisting they could turn me straight if I just gave them the chance. They wouldn't take no for an answer. I still wonder what they would've done had another kid not walked by and seen them. They got spooked and backed off."

"I had an old friend from another school: a guy," Violet added while I was still trying to absorb Jessa's story, "who messaged me online to tell me he thought I was really brave and that if I ever had any problems I should tell him and he'd stick up for me because he knew what it was like to get picked on. It was really sweet, actually. Cut to three months later and we've been in touch for a while; he gets drunk and tells me all about how I need to come visit him and smoke a joint or drink with him and then try having sex with him because he's *different* and I should try everything once."

"All of us have stories like that," Hattie added. "So you're not alone."

"And we all have stories about getting picked on, or getting beaten up or called names," Henry added. "I've been called a faggot dozens of times. That doesn't make it hurt any less when it happens, but I guess at some point you just have to realize that there are a lot of people who are ignorant out there, and that that's all they are. Just ignorant people. And we have each other to help us get through it."

"That's why we come here," Jake agreed. "To share our stories. So we can sit here in this circle and know we're not alone." He smiled. "So if you'd like to share... How has your first week been?"

I took them all in. All thirteen of them were watching me, and at my side, Sarah folded her hands in her lap and kept her eyes on her interlocked fingers. And it might seem strange, but for a moment, I forgot I wasn't gay. I'd only been fake-gay for a week, but sitting there with them, having walked in their shoes for the past seven days, I felt just as much a part of the group as any of them did.

"Well," I said, thinking only for a moment before I began, "I guess one thing that kind of hurt was that there was this girl I used to wave to every other day or so when we'd see each other between classes..."

Sarah and I were only alone for a few seconds after the meeting, between Jake saying goodbye to us by Sarah's car and Jessa coming up to us to offer her version of an apology, but those few seconds were so uncomfortable that Jessa was actually a welcome distraction.

"Hey," she began, a thin smile on her lips. "I guess... I don't know, maybe I should say sorry?"

"Maybe," Sarah replied, playing the role of affronted victim calculatingly well. Jessa pressed her lips together tightly for a moment, and I stayed silent.

"Look," she finally continued, "I don't know what I saw the other day anymore. Maybe I misinterpreted it. Maybe I didn't. If I did; if there's something I missed, then I'm sorry. But if I didn't, you guys are gonna have a lot to own up to when the truth comes out." She smirked. "And if I didn't... have a fun, not-awkward-at-all drive home after that *very* convincing kiss."

She stalked away without further ado, and once she was out of earshot, I didn't even make eye contact with Sarah before declaring, "I'm gonna walk home."

"Katie, c'mon," she countered hastily, grabbing my arm before I could leave. "Don't be ridiculous."

"Ridiculous?" I glared at her. "You wanna talk ridiculous right now? Seriously?"

"It was the only way!"

"Then we should've told the truth."

"Why? That was really cool in there, what just happened at the end. We were all getting along, and you wish we'd told the truth and made them hate us?"

"So instead you haul off and kiss me. Because that makes sense," I countered. "We agreed we weren't gonna do that."

"Desperate times call for desperate measures," Sarah said. "We were backed into a corner."

"And whose fault was that? Who spent four days making all of the decisions without telling me anything?"

"I thought I had it covered."

"You always do."

I turned and started to storm off, but she caught my arm again. "What's that supposed to mean?"

"It means we only do what you want and in the way that you want. Aren't we supposed to be in this together?"

"Not if you're gonna ruin everything at the first sign of trouble."

"Ruin everything," I echoed with a roll of my eyes. "Really, Sarah. *Everything*? So by that do you mean *your* reputation, *mine*, or your chances with a stupid boy?"

"He's not stupid, and all three."

"You don't even know him."

"And you do?"

I shook my head at her in disbelief, then threw my hands into the air and turned to walk away. "No, I don't. And apparently I don't know you, either."

"You're really gonna freak out like this over one kiss?" she called after me, and I knew she'd missed my point entirely. I didn't bother with a response.

I walked home. When I got there, I was already drying several of my own tears, and my mom took one look at me and knew that this time I *was* actually fighting with Sarah.

"Honey, what happened?" she tried to ask, but I ignored her and shut myself up in my room. That was where I stayed for the rest of the night, crying into my pillow and wondering why kissing Sarah just once had felt better than all of the hundreds of times I'd kissed Austin combined.

Chapter Six

I claimed illness the next day to avoid going to school and seeing Sarah, and Mom let me get away with it, especially after our talk over the weekend about how much rougher things had been for me lately. I sensed she wanted to take off work to spend the day interrogating me about what had gone wrong this time, because there was no doubt her "something is wrong in the world of Sarah and Katie" senses were tingling. But as it was, I ended up home alone and in bed, eating ice cream and watching the second episode of freaking *The L Word* because I wanted to know if Jenny was still into Tim or if she was already switching teams for Marina this early on.

I was halfway through when the doorbell rang. When I checked through the window by the door and saw it was Sarah, I almost didn't answer, but then I realized that if she was here she probably knew I was home, and, being Sarah, wouldn't give up until I answered.

I set my expression to a glare and then opened the door, but it was hard to stay angry when she was staring at me so hopefully on the other side of the threshold. "I know I screwed up," she began, and I groaned aloud and opened the door wider, then left it that way to pad into the kitchen. I heard her trail in behind me and close the door behind herself as I moved to make myself a bowl of cereal.

"Why aren't you at school, Sarah?" I asked her.

"Because I knew you wouldn't be."

"So why are you here?" I glanced at her as I poured milk into the bowl.

"Because," she sighed out, "I wanted to fix things, obviously. You know it's like... the planets are out of alignment when we're fighting."

"Who says we're fighting?"

"Don't be passive aggressive," she demanded. "You're angry at me for..." She looked around, and then lowered her voice. "For kissing you."

"There's no one home," I told her stoically. "And I don't want to talk about the kiss."

"Why not? It happened. We can't just not talk about it."

"That's exactly what we can and will do," I decided, and sat down at the table with my cereal.

"I don't think that's fair," she said, joining me. "Look, I can admit I screwed up. I wanna fix it. That involves talking stuff out." She chewed on her lip for a moment, and for the first time, she looked *really* nervous. The most nervous I'd seen her in a while. "Katie, I don't know about you, but... when we kissed, I-"

"I want," I interrupted, using a spoon to spool milk over a few dry bits of my cereal, "... I wanna be the one making the decisions from now on. That's what I think."

"Shouldn't we split them?" she asked, looking perturbed. "Like a compromise?"

"Yeah. But I want final say. Clearly my comfort level is way lower than yours, so rather than pushing my boundaries, I'll just set them, because you've set the bar way too high for me."

"How is that a compromise?"

"Well, you get to keep this fake couple thing going to get your guy, and I get to set the terms since I'm literally getting nothing out of this anyway."

She opened and closed her mouth for a moment, tracing shapes on the table with her finger. "I... I just feel like you're doing this out of anger."

"Yeah, a little bit," I admitted. "Can you blame me?"

"I just don't understand why you're being so defensive. I skipped school to come apologize to you and to try and work things out. I think that I have some valid points here if you'd just listen."

"Like what? Go ahead, then."

"Well." She took a deep breath. "We kissed. And I know we said we didn't want to, but it helped a lot with Jessa, and... I think it could be something we might wanna do in the future-"

"No way."

"Just every now and then. Just to keep the illusion going."

"Nope." I closed my lips over my spoon, then removed it from my mouth and pointed it at her accusingly. With my mouth comically full, I declared, trying to break the tension, "You just want an excuse to kiss me again."

She rolled her eyes, but the corners of her lips tugged upwards, and I knew she could tell I was starting to defrost a little. "Obviously. At the very least, I think we went about this the wrong way. I should be more focused on you and less on Sam. He's already noticed us; the rest will come naturally from him if he's interested. I'll play hard to get and be hopelessly devoted to you, Katie Hammontree."

"That sounds absolutely terrible," I told her. "Just awful."

"I'm sure. Me carrying your books everywhere, telling you how pretty you are, waiting on you hand and foot..."

"Horrifying." I nodded at her and raised another spoonful of cereal to my mouth as she grinned. I smiled back at her once I'd gotten the cereal into my mouth, and felt some milk dribble down my chin. She laughed and reached out to wipe it away.

"And apparently you need me, anyway." With the milk gone, she tapped at my chin once with her thumb and then took her hand away. She'd done it before in the past, but something about it felt a little different now.

We were quiet for a moment, and then she let out a heavy sigh and cupped her cheek in one hand, resting her elbow on the table. "Well, at least you're a good kisser."

"Don't even start," I warned her, but she was already grinning again.

"Am I? C'mon, you can tell me. I know I am."

"You're so full of yourself."

"That doesn't make me any less of a good kisser. Seriously though, you made kissing a girl strangely pleasant."

"You're too honest sometimes."

"I know." She shrugged her shoulders. "My parents say it's a gift and a curse."

"I... Okay, you know what?" I let out a sigh and shook my head, aware that I'd probably regret this.

"How about this? If I call all of the shots from now on, you can be responsible for making us a convincing couple, considering you have way more experience with actually being part of a couple. But you have to get my approval first."

"Done deal." She smiled at me. "Easy."

"Alright, then." I took the last bite of my food and then offered her my hand to shake. "Let's be the best lesbian couple we can be, then. We might as well, now that we're in this deep."

"You got it, girlfriend. Time to take this school by storm," she agreed, and we shook on it.

Things changed rather quickly between Sarah and me after that.

We were friends by night, and a couple by day, and things that'd started out as "Sarah and Katie coupley things" quickly wormed their way into our "friendly things". Sarah spent a week taking my hand in hers and rubbing her thumb along my fingers whenever I got nervous at school, say, right before a test or whenever we were being teased or harassed in some way, and so on Day Fifteen of our new arrangement, when we were alone in my bedroom and I had a test I was trying my hardest to cram for, her hand was suddenly in mine and her thumb was caressing my fingers, and I didn't think anything of it until long after she was gone.

Stuff like that happened constantly, and not just with touching. Kissing became a semi-regular thing, and it took me much longer to get comfortable with it than it took Sarah, even though we'd agreed to only pecks for now. She'd kissed a lot of people, and I'd hoped that me being the first *girl* she'd kissed might slow down the progression a little bit and leave us both on the same page, but for some reason she pretty much just dove into being physically affectionate with me and never looked back.

We pecked in hallways between classes, mostly, which was my preference, were I to choose between that and the kind of kissing we'd done at the LAMBDA meeting. Kissing Sarah was fairly pleasant, but *really* kissing her ultimately did my brain and body more harm than good and made me feel things I wasn't comfortable nor used to feeling.

We went to another two LAMBDA meetings, and even as Jessa slowly began to ease off of Sarah and me, Jake, Hattie, and Violet emerged as three people we really got along well with. All thirteen of them were nice for the most part, though, and all of them had something we could talk to them about. Being gay was like that; you could have nothing in common with someone, but the gay thing was always there to fall back on. For me and Sarah, it just meant falling back on our original fake stories we'd told.

Two and a half weeks after our first kiss, Sarah surprised me at lunch with a folded piece of paper in her hand. She and Hannah bore matching grins as she handed it over to me and announced, "Guys, look at what we're doing tomorrow night."

I unfolded the paper and took in the colorful writing on it. "Justin Barnes is having a party," I announced, struggling to sound enthusiastic. "Cool." He was a football player, which probably meant a night of booze and debauchery. I knew Sarah was probably aching for a party at this point after over a month of nothing, so there was no doubt she'd be dragging me along.

"Awesome." Connor grinned, leaning over to examine the paper in my hands. "I'm there. Who else is in?"

"Everyone, of course," Sarah replied. "The whole school should be there, for the most part. Justin throws the biggest parties of the year. Graham and Bonnie, you guys are going, too."

"Hey, I'm not complaining," Graham agreed, raising his hands in the air defensively. "I just can't get caught with alcohol on my breath again. I'll drive."

"Perfect. You're the only one with a car big enough to hold all of us, anyway," Hannah said.

And *that* was how on Friday I found myself squished between Dina and Sarah in the middle row of Graham's eight-person SUV around nine thirty at night. I felt bad telling my parents I was spending the night at Sarah's, but it wasn't like that was necessarily a lie. I *was* going to spend the night at Sarah's. There was just a small stop in between that I'd failed to mention.

Justin Barnes's house was kind of huge. The only person I knew who lived in a house bigger than his was Sarah, in fact. It was three stories high and already filled to the brim with teenagers, and I could hear the music blasting from all the way down the street. I wondered briefly if the neighbors would wind up calling the police because of the noise, but then I realized that in this particular neighborhood, the houses were spaced further apart. Justin's was one of only three on his entire street, and the music was faint as we passed by his neighbor.

Graham parked on the side of the road and we agreed to meet back at his car at eleven-thirty, to give him time to get everyone home before midnight. We split up pretty quickly after we got inside: Dina and Josephine grabbed Bonnie with the intention of forcing her to dance, Connor and Graham went off somewhere – most likely to scope out girls to hit on – and Hannah left to grab a drink and then mingle with the rest of her other friends on the football team and the cheerleading squad.

That left Sarah and I alone to get drinks by ourselves, and although she didn't bring up Sam at first, I could see her scoping out the other people at the party like she was looking for someone.

"Do you think Sam is here?" I finally asked her, as we stood together near the wall of Justin's living room, sipping our drinks and watching the crowd of dancers in the center of the room. I mostly watched Dina, Josephine, and Bonnie, who looked like they were having fun in the center of the crowd.

"I don't know," Sarah said. "But I'm sticking to the plan either way: don't approach; *be* approached." She smirked at me. "Besides, I can't do anything with him here, anyway. At least not in front of everyone. I'm here with you."

"Plenty of empty rooms," I pointed out, not really meaning it, and she laughed.

"Yeah, I guess. We'll see."

We fell silent as I scanned the room for another moment. Right around the time I finally found Sam, sitting in a circle off to the side and seemingly engaged of a game of Spin the Bottle, Sarah nudged me and pointed straight ahead of us. "Hey, look," she said.

I followed her gaze and my eyes landed on Austin, front to back with another girl amongst the crowd of dancers, his hands tight on her waist. I didn't know how to feel about that. I wasn't upset, but it was strange to see him with someone else. I wondered idly how much he'd had to drink; he'd always been shy about dancing with me.

"We should do something fun," Sarah declared, and downed the rest of her drink. "Wanna dance?" she asked as she set her empty cup aside.

A brief image flashed in the back of my brain: Sarah and I, pressed together the way Austin was pressed against the mystery girl with him, swaying to the beat of a heavy bass with fuzzy minds and wandering hands.

"No thanks," I barely managed to get out. She sighed heavily.

"Why not? You need to come out of your shell a little. It'll be fun!"

"Sam's playing Spin the Bottle," was my response. I nodded in the appropriate direction, and she turned. "If you hurry, you might be able to kiss him."

I watched her take in the circle of people for a moment, and could practically see the wheels turning in her head. Relieved that I'd distracted her, I let myself relax a little, and finished my first drink. It was strong, and it took me a moment to get it all down, so by the time I'd set it aside, she was facing me again, a small smile on her lips.

"So, that dance, then?" she asked, and offered me her hand. My lips parted in surprise, and I looked past her, to Sam and the others.

"But Sam-" I tried, and she cut me off before I could finish.

"Sam's not my concern tonight." She looked down at her hand for emphasis. "C'mon. I'll teach you to grind."

"Are you serious?" I asked, flushing. "I've done it before."

"With *that* doesn't count," she said, tilting her head in Austin's direction. "He's terrible. Like, I feel really sorry for that girl he's with right now."

"He wasn't that bad," I argued, mostly to keep her distracted. I didn't know what was good and what was bad, honestly. I thought about offering to get her another drink to bide some time.

"He was bad," she retorted, and, sick of my stalling, reached over to grasp my hand with hers. "Look, let's call it what it was back in LAMBDA two weeks ago: We've made out. And we've been dating for a while, haven't we? There's no going back at this point, and if you're as dedicated to acting like a couple as I am, you'd dance with me, since it's not like I can get away with dancing with anyone else anyway. C'mon." She winked at me. "I'll try not to get you too hot and bothered."

I rolled my eyes at her, fighting off another blush. "Trust me, we're good there."

"Then what're you scared of?" She tightened her grip on my hand subtly and tugged me gently toward the dance floor.

And I've never been happier to see Connor in my life than I was right then, when he came at us out of nowhere and planted his feet right between us from behind, then threw an arm around both of our shoulders. I could smell the alcohol on his breath as he announced, "I love you guys! Seriously, screw Hannah. Like, you two are where it's at."

Sarah and I exchanged knowing looks. Poor Connor. Rejected *again.*

"I agree," I told him, offering Sarah a sickeningly sweet smile. "You know, you two should definitely go play Spin the Bottle together. They're doing it right over there."

"Actually, you and I were going to dance, Katie," Sarah shot back, but Connor'd already lit up at my idea.

"Yeah! Katie, come play with us, too. It'll be fun!"

I immediately looked panic-stricken. "Actually, maybe I should go dance, after all. I think Dina and Josephine are in that crowd somewhere with Bonnie. You guys go ahead, though." I moved to leave, but Sarah grabbed my arm to keep me in place.

"Oh, no you don't," she said, smirking at me. "If we're going, you're coming with us."

And just like that, Connor was leading us over to the circle that'd formed. When Sam and the others saw we were joining, they clapped encouragingly, and I found myself being handed a beer as I took a seat. Sarah and Connor sat down on my other side, and I avoided Sam's eyes, but felt his gaze on us along with the rest of the group.

A girl with blonde hair that I recognized from the cheerleading squad offered Connor the empty bottle. Christine Goddard. "You guys start the next round off," she suggested. "Girls have to kiss girls, but guys don't have to kiss guys." She eyed Sarah and me and then said, in a tone that made me think it wasn't intended as a friendly jab, "That shouldn't be a problem for you two, I assume."

If Sarah heard the taunting in her voice, she ignored it. "If girls are kissing girls, it only seems fair that it should be the same for the guys," she teased.

"Nobody wants to see dudes kissing," one of the other boys countered, and Connor abruptly spun the bottle a little too roughly, his coordination off after what had obviously been quite a few drinks. It landed on some poor girl I didn't know, who ended up on the receiving end of a sloppy kiss from Connor. She wiped at her mouth, her nose wrinkling in displeasure as I was handed the bottle.

"You're the lesbian, right?" the boy sitting next to Sam asked. I nodded, almost afraid of what he'd say next, but he grinned and just replied, "Awesome. Here's to you getting a chick." Then he tipped the bottle in his hand back and downed the rest of his beer.

I set my own bottle down and was just about to spin it, when a new voice just behind Sam asked, "Hey, mind if I join?"

I looked up and saw Jessa standing over our group, a drink in her hand. I was too busy being surprised she was here at the party to notice what was said, but a moment later, she was seated across from me in the circle and waiting patiently for me to spin. I felt Sarah tense beside me. Even if Jessa had become nicer over the past couple of weeks, Sarah's dislike of her hadn't lessened. But I didn't mind Jessa, even if I was still a little wary of her. She'd been right about Sarah and me. Sarah just hated the idea of not being able to outsmart someone.

"Go," Christine urged me, sounding impatient. I spun the bottle hastily, and it rotated wildly across the floor, finally slowing to a stop on Jessa.

I looked up at her to see she had both eyebrows raised. She looked excited at the prospect of kissing me, and I wasn't sure how to feel about that. "Cool. Katie's cute," she said, shooting me a smile that felt more like a smirk. I glanced at Sarah, but her eyes were trained on the ground. Her jaw looked a little tighter than usual, and I knew she was upset that someone who appeared to be her girlfriend was meant to kiss someone she didn't like.

I looked back at Jessa, overly aware of everyone watching us as she moved first, crawling on her hands and knees across the circle to place herself in front of me. I sat, unmoving, as she wordlessly took my chin in her hands and guided her mouth to mine.

My hands stayed at my sides as we kissed, and while I was acutely aware of a few whistles and clapping from the guys in the circle as her lips moved over mine, I was mostly stuck in my own head, mentally comparing her to Sarah. Jessa and Sarah both knew how to kiss, and they both left my heart pounding and my lips buzzing, but kissing Jessa was mostly nothing like it'd been with Sarah, and I could tell that she was only enjoying kissing me because Sarah was watching.

She pulled away after a few seconds, and I blinked repeatedly as she swept a finger under my chin and then returned to her spot in the circle, that smug smile back on her lips again. We got a few more claps as Sarah grabbed at the bottle, and I tried to clear my fuzzy head – both from the kiss and the alcohol – as I watched her take her time. I wondered for a moment if she knew something I didn't about rigging the bottle, and if she was trying to figure out how to get it to land on Sam. Sarah was a smart girl when it came to anything academic, with the exception of a couple of the sciences. I couldn't remember at the moment if Physics was one of them.

Finally, her jaw tightened again, and instead of spinning the bottle, she twisted it back as though she was about to spin it, and then abruptly twisted it all the way around, her grip tight on it. When it was pointed at me, she released it, and dared anyone to challenge her. No one said a word, beyond a few shared grins and some raised eyebrows, and I barely had time to wonder why she'd given up a shot at kissing Sam before she'd taken my face in her hands and I was suddenly being kissed again.

I'd spent the weeks following our first kiss convincing myself that it was an anomaly; a fluke kiss that'd only been so good because it'd taken me by surprise. And thank God I was able to use that excuse for this one, too, because it was just as good as the first.

With Jessa, I'd kept my hands at my sides, but with Sarah, they flew right to her body like they belonged there, starting on where her thighs rested between us and then slipping to her sides by the time one of her hands had moved to my neck.

She deepened the kiss quickly, lips moving gently against mine, and I felt her pull me closer as her tongue sent sparks straight to behind my eyelids. My stomach churned and flopped and for the first time, I was sure I knew what people meant when they talked about another person giving them butterflies.

We weren't anywhere near done when I vaguely registered someone saying, "Oh, man, that's hot," and remembered where we were. In an instant, I'd pulled away, and Sarah blinked at me, looking just as dazed as I was. I felt my cheeks burn and my stomach turn unpleasantly, that comment ringing in my head, and I couldn't bear to look at anyone else in the circle, but Sarah's eyes held my focus anyway as they slowly lost their glazed look. She swallowed once, visibly, and then her hand moved down to grip mine.

"C'mon," she said, firmly, and then she was tugging me to my feet and pulling me out of the circle and through the living room.

I followed, confused and a little tipsy as the drinks I'd had began to take their effect. Sarah, too, was obviously not sober, because she wasn't quite walking straight as she led me. "Where are we going?" I asked her, but she pulled me down a hallway without answering, trying a couple of doors before she finally found one that opened. A second later, I'd been yanked inside a bedroom and the door was shut behind us.

I stared at Sarah, growing even more confused as she rounded on me and moved back toward me. Her lips were on mine again before I could register that she'd moved close enough to kiss me, and my eyes fluttered shut even as my eyebrows furrowed. It was hard to think now that the alcohol was taking over my senses, but my body thought it'd be a good idea to kiss her back, and what section of my brain was still operating agreed with that decision until right around the time I realized that we were alone.

We were *alone*. Why were we kissing if we were alone?

I stopped thinking about that when I remembered how good kissing Sarah felt, and then my lips were moving against hers fervently, my eyes squeezed shut as I gave up on rational thought. Sarah was kissing me and kissing Sarah felt great; *fantastic* even, and that was all that mattered.

But we were both drunk. And still alone. And we were both girls who were supposed to be straight. This was not very straight.

I gasped when her tongue ran along my lip, squeezed my eyes shut so tightly it started to hurt, and then forced myself to gently push her away.

She opened her eyes and I watched them struggle to focus on me. Her lips were swollen from kissing me and she was breathing hard, and in that two seconds before exactly what we were doing really hit me, I think I'd have died to see her like that over and over again.

But then those two seconds passed, and we were two drunk best friends who'd just fooled around in a bedroom whose owner we'd probably never met. I swallowed hard, trying to stop seeing double, and at last, declared, "So I think I'm really drunk right now."

Sarah licked her lips even as her eyes fell to mine. "Yeah," she breathed out. Then she tilted her head to the side, and told me, matter-of-fact-ly, "I like kissing you."

"I like kissing you, too, Sarah," I agreed amiably, nodding my head, and we stared at each other for another long moment.

Then the corners of her lips tilted upward, and suddenly, we were both slumped against the wall side by side, giggling hard until our stomachs started to hurt.

We stumbled out of the bedroom together at some point soon after that, and the next morning, I'd remember thinking, right then, that I'd definitely not been drunk enough for what'd just happened, and that more alcohol sounded like a good idea.

And then I wouldn't remember much after that.

I woke up in Sarah's massive king bed the next morning with a pounding head. Sarah wasn't with me, but the mystery of where she'd gone was solved within a few seconds, because she came back into the bedroom a moment later with a water bottle in each hand. I realized that her getting out of bed was probably what had woken me up in the first place.

"Hey, you're up," she croaked, her mouth and throat sounding as dry as mine felt. I accepted the water bottle from her thankfully and downed half of it while she sipped from her own. When I was finished, I set it aside and blinked the sleep out of my eyes as I rubbed at my head.

"Dude, I can't remember most of last night," I realized, alarmed. "What happened?"

"God, where do I begin?" she mumbled, collapsing back on the bed next to me. "I'm trying to remember myself. I just know you got wasted and Dina and Josephine had to help us up to my room."

"Well, that's embarrassing."

"Yeah," Sarah sighed out. "Let's never drink that much again. I think I was pretty bad too; you just got bad a little quicker than I did."

I closed my eyes and wracked my brain for memories. I had everything up until kissing Sarah in the bedroom, but I was perfectly content to lose that memory... or at least act like I had and then never mention it again. There was something about dancing with Josephine, Dina, and Bonnie at some point afterward, and then trying to cheer up an upset Connor, I think... *and* there was something about Sarah and Sam in there, but I didn't know what.

"You hooked up with Sam," I guessed, glancing over at her. "Congrats."

"No, I don't think so," she disagreed, shaking her head. "I just remember talking to him for a while. I think you were dancing."

"Well, that's still good." I started to get out of bed, feeling her eyes on me as I reached for my water bottle. I needed to use the bathroom.

"Is it?" she asked me. I turned, my hand on the knob of her bedroom door, to see her staring at me, eyebrows furrowed, from her spot on her bed. I didn't want to think about why she'd ask me that.

"Yeah," I said, and then left the room.

I had to stay at Sarah's for a little while to make sure I felt one-hundred percent recovered so that there was no evidence of where I'd been last night. But once I was feeling better, she took me home and dropped me off. My parents were waiting inside for me: Dad in the kitchen reading the paper, and Mom working on brunch.

"Hey honey, did you have a good time with Sarah? I could use some help with cooking, if you're up for it," Mom said.

"It was fun," I lied. "We actually stayed up until, like, five in the morning, so I think I might go back to sleep, actually."

"Oh, okay." Mom sounded intrigued more than disappointed, and I saw her and dad exchange a look. "What'd you two do all night?"

"Um, just talked and stuff." I shrugged my shoulders.

"Okay," Mom repeated, and I went to my room.

Once I was there, I took out my phone and exchanged a few texts with both Dina and Josephine, who I'd sent about a thousand thank-you texts to earlier after what Sarah'd told me they'd done. They both seemed amused more than anything, which was nice, but I was still really embarrassed. Last night hadn't been like me; I'd never really been anything more than tipsy before, and I vowed right then to never drink that much again.

I leaned forward as I sat in my bed, closing my eyes and resting my head in my hands. Everything felt confusing now, and I just wanted this thing with Sarah to end before I wound up more frazzled than I could handle. But it wouldn't end. We still had over seven months left to go.

"It's fake, it's fake, it's fake," I murmured over and over again, and then I laid down, and, at some point, mercifully fell back to sleep.

Chapter Seven

LAMBDA's first out-of-school meeting was the following Tuesday. Rather than sitting in our usual circle in room 405, we all carpooled to a place about ten minutes away, which Jake described as "Flowery Branch's local LGBT resource center". I hadn't known such a place existed, and Sarah expressed the same ignorance as we drove there.

With Sarah and I included, there were fifteen people in our club, and we all gathered inside the building – which featured a small rainbow flag outside its front door – to have a talk with a man named Owen Bradshaw, although he told us immediately that he preferred to just be called by his first name. He was in his late twenties and worked at the center.

"Our general mission is to make sure the local LGBT youth... or, in other words, you guys," he said, "feel comfortable having a place to come to when you need somewhere to turn, whether it's for answers to questions or if you have family issues and don't feel comfortable returning home. We've housed teens overnight, and we've also given them hot meals. But for less serious circumstances, we've had people stop by just to borrow a good book or a movie from our collection over on that shelf."

He pointed across the lobby, to a bookshelf filled to the brim with DVDs and novels. I raised both eyebrows, surprised there were enough to fill the shelf. It'd been like pulling teeth for Sarah and me to try and find any books or movies a couple of weeks ago.

"So, anyway, why *you* guys are here. We were contacted by Jake about some of you potentially being unaware that we were here, although I will say I do see a few familiar faces amongst you." He smiled. "Additionally, we've decided we'd like to do something small for National Coming Out Day, which is coming up when?"

Owen raised a hand to his ear expectantly, and the rest of the group chorused, "October 11th!" as Sarah and I stood dumbly amongst them.

"Right. So, for today, just feel free to explore, look around, talk amongst yourselves... and I'm sure Jake will keep you posted, but we'll probably meet back here in a few days on Sunday the 10th and work out what we'll be doing on the 11th. Let me know if you guys have any questions or need anything. We've got some food out on the table over there if you're hungry; help yourselves."

Our group of fifteen immediately dissolved into several familiar cliques. Henry, Hattie, and Jessa headed for the buffet table with some others, and I saw Jake stay back to talk to Owen.

"Let's go look at the shelf," Sarah suggested, looking genuinely excited at the prospect. "We can see if there's anything good we haven't heard of."

"Why?" I asked, raising an eyebrow and following her anyway. "Are you gonna actually read another book?"

"Maybe." She knelt down by the shelf and I watched her, surprised by her answer. "I mean, the first one I read was decent, minus the ending. Maybe I'll find one that has a happy ending." She picked out a book that caught her eye, and grinned. "Holy crap. Look, Katie... lesbian *erotica*."

"Put that back," I hissed, but she waved it in my face, still grinning.

"I should definitely borrow this. I mean, *you* aren't taking care of me sexually so I've gotta pick up the slack somehow now that I'm no longer sleeping with boys, either."

"Gross. I do not need to know about your high sex drive."

"Hey, girls." I jumped abruptly at the sound of Owen's voice, and turned to see him approaching us. "See anything you're interested in? If you want to check out a book or a movie, all you have to do is sign your name, phone number, email, and the item of your choice on that sheet over there." He pointed to a desk just a few feet away, and Sarah looked over at it with interest. I realized pretty quickly that it wasn't the sheet that'd caught her eye, but what was stacked next it.

"Wait, are those condoms?" she asked.

"Yes," Owen said. "We always have free condoms available to promote safe sex. Feel free to take one."

"Oh, no." Sarah waved him away quickly. "No need for those with this one." She tilted her head toward me, and Owen smiled at us.

"Well, feel free to keep browsing. Just let me know if you end up signing anything out."

"We will," Sarah agreed. Once he'd left and she was sure no one was looking, she leaned over and stole a condom.

I rolled my eyes at her. "I thought you couldn't sleep with boys anymore because you're with me?"

She smirked at me. "Doesn't hurt to be prepared. After all, I *am* talking to Sam, now."

It was true. After whatever'd happened at the party Friday, Sam and Sarah had begun texting casually, and both yesterday and today, he'd talked to her in their English class. It was risky to call it this early on, but it seemed like she had his attention now and that they were well on their way to a hookup. I wasn't sure how to feel about that. I guess it was good that Sarah'd probably get what she'd wanted from the beginning, but the closer she got to achieving that goal, the more used I felt.

It was safe to say now that if it weren't for Jake and the rest of the LAMBDA club, I'd end our fake relationship and come clean. But I genuinely liked them all – with the exception of Jessa, who I was still a little cool toward after Friday. Still, I didn't want her or any of the others to hate me.

I wandered away from Sarah to where Violet was sitting in one of the lounge chairs, flipping through an issue of "Out" magazine that'd been lying on one of the end tables beside her. She looked up at me and smiled. "Hey," she said.

"Hey." I took a seat next to her and leaned over to look at the magazine. On one page was a picture of a Pride parade in New York; on the other, a news story on the latest state to legalize gay marriage. "Have you been here before?" I asked her.

She nodded. "Yeah, a couple of times." She hesitated for a moment, and then explained, "Things were a little rough between my parents and

I right after I came out to them. I stayed here for a night."

"Wow," I breathed out. I knew, of course, that there were parents out there who reacted badly to having a gay child, but it was so hard to imagine it when I knew it would be such a non-issue with mine.

"How did you parents react when you told them?" she asked me.

I colored slightly. "Oh... I haven't told them."

She set the magazine aside, curious now. "Why? Do you think they'll be upset?"

"No." I shook my head. "My uncle's gay, so I know they'll be fine."

"Then why haven't you told them?" she asked, confused. I opened and closed my mouth for a moment, struggling for an answer, but Sarah saved me by plopping down on my other side, a book in her hand.

"Hello, ladies."

I shot her a knowing look. "You didn't."

"I did. Already signed the sheet." She waved the book in my face, and I rolled my eyes at her as Violet watched the both of us.

"You got the erotica, didn't you?"

"No!" Sarah retorted, defensive. "I was just kidding about that."

"Shame," I sighed out. "You could've used the sex tips."

"Hey!" she replied, mock-offended, and I grinned at her until she slapped at my arm.

"Ow!" I grabbed for her hand, but she pulled it out of my reach, smirking at me.

On my other side, Violet smiled widely at us and said, "Aww... you guys are so cute together. Stop it; you're making me sad I don't have anyone."

My smile died a little and I turned away from Sarah, facing Violet again. Eager to change the subject, I asked, "What about you and Hattie? I see you guys hanging out sometimes."

Violet shook her head, looking a little embarrassed. "Um... yeah, we kind of tried it last year, but it didn't work out. I'm lucky we made it out of that one with an intact friendship."

"Well, you can't go wrong with any of the girls here as long as you don't pick Jessa," Sarah told her, rolling her eyes.

"She's not my type," Violet dismissed. "I mean, what she did to you guys... I thought that was really weird and uncalled for. She's, like, way too abrasive for me."

I searched the room briefly for Jessa and found her still talking to Henry by the buffet table. She must've sensed I was staring at her, because after a moment, she turned to look back at me, and then winked. Sarah's hand, which had moved to rest on my shoulder at some point, fleetingly tightened its grip, and I realize she'd been watching Jessa, too. That explained the wink.

"You know what I don't get," I finally said. "If she doesn't think we're faking it anymore, then she has no reason to have any ill will toward us, and if she *does* still think we're faking it, then she should think flirting with me wouldn't piss you off, right?" I looked to Sarah for confirmation, but Violet, instead, was the one who answered.

"Jessa's kind of strong-willed. She'll probably never be fully willing to admit she was wrong... even to herself."

"She hates me for showing her up," Sarah said. "Now I'm glad I got that jab in about her not having a girlfriend."

"In retrospect, it was deserved," I said, playing along. "Anyway, tell me about your book."

She flashed the cover at me. "Pretty basic. Girl meets girl, girls fall in love, and as far as I know, no one dies or goes back to men or gets pregnant, or any combination of the three. I'm determined to get my happy ending."

"You really are big on them, aren't you?" I asked her. Sarah nodded proudly and tucked the book into the bag hanging off of her shoulder.

"That I am," she confirmed. "I won't stop until I get one."

"Good luck," Violet cut in, grinning. "We don't get them often."

"So how was your club meeting?" Mom asked me at dinner later that night. "Did you do anything interesting?"

"Yeah." I nodded at her. "We visited an animal shelter."

"That sounds fun," Dad said. "What kinds of animals did they have?"

"Oh, just the usual. Dogs, cats, birds, fish... it was like a zoo in there. It was kind of tempting to just take them all home with me."

Mom smiled over at me. "We'd forgive you if you did. I'm sure they were adorable, honey."

I let out a short laugh. "So you'd still love me even if I brought a random dog home?"

"Of course." There was a short pause, and Mom added, "A dog... a cat... *both*, neither... we'd love you regardless."

I paused to stare at her, my fork stilling over my plate as Mom's eyes stayed resolutely glued to hers. She took a piece of the steak she'd cooked and brought it to her mouth, and her gaze shifted to Dad as she chewed. He scooped up a spoonful of mashed potatoes and glanced back at her.

I set my fork down, suddenly not hungry. "Maybe I be excused," I deadpanned, and then got up without waiting for an answer.

I heard the sound of a chair scraping against the floor behind me, and then my mom called, "Honey!" but I was already gone.

I slammed my bedroom door shut behind myself, locked it, and immediately grabbed my phone and called Sarah. "Pick up, pick up," I murmured, and let out a sigh of relief when I heard the click of her answering.

"Hello?"

"Sarah, my parents know," I said quickly. I could feel myself beginning to panic.

"What? What do you mean?"

"I mean they *know*," I emphasized. "They know that I'm fake-gay, but they think I'm actually gay. I don't know what to do. I think I'm about to have a panic attack."

"Wait, calm down, Katie. How do they know?"

"I don't know! I didn't do anything differently, I swear! I didn't say or do anything! They just do!"

"Are you sure?"

"Yes! They know I didn't really join a club for animals; I think they might even know it's a gay club. They asked me how it went and started using freaking metaphors about how they'd love me whether I brought home a cat or a dog."

"Shit," Sarah breathed out, and then seemed to collect herself. "Okay, listen. Katie, they already told you they'd love you regardless. So the worst won't happen, right?"

"Except I can't tell them I'm gay when I'm not!" I pointed out, my voice rising. "What the hell?!"

To my surprise, Sarah replied, "Yeah, okay."

I paused, momentarily calm. "Wait. *Okay?*"

"Yeah. They're your parents, not just kids we go to school with. They're family. If you think telling them the truth is the best decision, I'm not gonna tell you to lie to them. But you aren't gonna call this off if they tell you to, right?" I was silent on the other end, honestly unsure of my answer, and she pressed, "Right, Katie?"

"Yeah," I agreed, nodding my head even though she couldn't see it. "Sure. Right. I don't have to take their advice, that's true. I'll just, you know..." I swallowed hard, "...be a total disappointment of a daughter until I tell everyone at school the truth. *Or* tell my parents I'm gay and go back on it later. Great."

"What are you gonna do?" she asked me, but there was a knock on my door before I could answer.

"Katie, we'd just like to talk," came my mom's voice.

I spoke quickly to Sarah, hissing, "I don't know what I should do."

"Maybe just let them do the talking first?" she suggested. A harder knock came on my door; this time I could tell it was my dad.

"Shit," I whispered, and abruptly hung up on Sarah. I crossed to the door, grit my teeth and shook my head, and then unlocked it and yanked it open.

My parents stood together on the other side, and my mom sighed with relief. "Can we talk?" she asked, and I nodded nervously and stepped back to let them inside. Mom motioned for me to take a seat on my bed, and then sat down next to me as Dad placed himself in the desk chair across the room.

"That was very insensitive and tactless of me," Mom told me, putting a hand over mine gently. "I wanted you to be able to tell me on your own time, but I thought... I guess I thought maybe you just needed to be sure that we were going to still love you."

I furrowed my eyebrows, unsure of how to respond to that. She was talking like she'd been thinking about this for longer than just a few weeks, or even a few months.

"Your mother had the best of intentions, Katie," Dad said next. "We've talked a lot about how my parents reacted to Kevin, and we wanted to make sure you weren't afraid you were going to go through that."

"How long have you been planning this?" I asked at last.

Mom gave a short laugh. "Oh, honey, we've had some idea since you were six. You were giving little girls flowers when we'd take you to the park. You picked so many of them we had to pay money to replace them."

"You were quite the charmer," Dad joked, and my mouth felt dry.

"I was?" I asked, feeling strangely empty.

"Yes. And it's been very hard, as a parent, trying to prepare for that. I wanted to do everything perfectly, and so did your dad. We wanted to do everything for you that wasn't done for Kevin. We even hoped he'd be around more to give you someone to look up to, but unfortunately that hasn't been the case." She sighed, and took my hand in hers. "Katie, we love you so, *so* much, and I couldn't bear the idea of you struggling for all of these years and worrying that we wouldn't still love you."

"I never thought you wouldn't love me," I interrupted quickly. This was a lot to take in, but I was glad she'd finally said something I had a response for. "I knew you'd be fine with it."

"Good," Dad said. "Then we did our job correctly."

"It wasn't easy," Mom added. "I've wanted to have this conversation with you for a very long time. I'd thought maybe you'd be ready for it soon, after the whole thing with Austin-"

"Wait," I interrupted. What they were telling me was finally beginning to sink in. "You thought- I mean, you knew while I was with Austin that-"

"That you were gay? Oh, absolutely, honey. I could see you weren't happy, and I could see the way you'd light up anytime you so much as mentioned Sarah's name."

"Huh." I stared at my feet, unable to really think of anything to say to that. "That's... huh."

"We just wanted to make sure you know that we love you, and that no matter who you love, that won't change," Dad told me, folding his hands in his lap. "You can be gay, or bisexual, or even straight, and we'll love you as long as you're being who you are, okay?"

"Okay." I paused, then looked up abruptly, glancing back and forth between the both of them. "Wait, you think I'm in love with Sarah?"

I could handle being mistaken for gay. Hell, I was pretty sure I could handle *being* gay, or even bisexual, if that was what I was. That wasn't nearly as much as a concern to me as being in love with my straight best friend.

Mom looked confused. "Aren't you? You two are inseparable."

"Because we've always been best friends," I insisted. "That's how being best friends works."

"Well…" Mom looked like she was struggling not to argue, "I guess if that's how you feel, honey, then it's not my place to say otherwise."

"But you want to," I accused. "You think I love her." I looked to Dad, who wouldn't quite look back at me. "You both do!"

"Well, you two *are* very close," he admitted.

"Because we're best friends!"

"Okay, sweetie." Mom patted me on the arm and got to her feet, ignoring that I was gaping at the both of them now. I let out a forced laugh as Dad got to his feet, too.

"Do you guys even have real jobs or lives, or do you just sit around and gossip about my love life all day?" I asked them, appalled.

Dad raised his hands defensively, already backing his way out of the room. "I'm gonna let your mom handle this one."

Mom bent over in front of me and gave me a kiss on the forehead. "Sarah's a great girl. I think you two would be very cute together."

"She's straight," I insisted, shooting her an incredulous look. She smiled back at me.

"I only have one biological child, but Sarah might as well be my second one. And a mother knows." She tapped her temple with a nod, and then kissed me on the forehead again. "If you need to talk, I'm always here."

"Oh my God," I murmured to myself, shaking my head as my mom closed the door on her way out. "They are literally insane."

I reached for my phone when it buzzed with a text from Sarah a moment later. *"R they still talking to u? Is everything ok?"*

I typed out a response, and sent, *"Uh, they've always known I liked girls?"*

My phone rang seconds after I'd sent the text, and I answered it to loud laughter and an incredulous, "What?!"

"You're telling me," I mumbled, shaking my head again. "I don't even know anymore. Whatever."

"Do they know we're dating?" she asked, amusement still audible in her voice.

"Nope," I said. "And we should probably keep it that way because I'm kind of afraid of what they'd say if they found out at this point."

"I know, right?"

We spent a few minutes laughing about my parents and how off-the-wall and weird they could be sometimes, and I didn't really give her the full story. I wasn't sure of what to make of it myself, let alone what Sarah'd make of it. So I dismissed it all and eventually ended my call with her, and tried to nap for the next hour.

I couldn't fall asleep. I kept thinking back to Austin, and the way we'd always felt more like friends forcing a relationship rather than a genuine couple with romantic feelings. But that didn't necessarily mean I was gay... and neither did handing out flowers to random girls at age six. Maybe I'd just wanted a friend. Maybe my parents were mistaken. They certainly were about *Sarah*, that was for sure, and about my being in love with her.

But I couldn't shake the tense feeling that grew in my chest the longer I mulled over what they'd said. Even if I didn't have feelings for any other girl in particular, I'd liked kissing both Jessa and Sarah more than I'd liked kissing Austin. Maybe Austin just wasn't the right guy for me... but what if that wasn't it? What if my perfect boyfriend was actually a girlfriend? And how on earth was I supposed to know if that was the case?

I chewed on my lip as I laid in bed, and, finally, I made a decision.

Tomorrow, I'd pay Owen and the LGBT resource center another visit.

Chapter Eight

Lunch the next day marked the third straight school day of Connor acting unnaturally subdued. Ever since the party, he'd sat silently for the majority of the period and repeatedly shot me furtive looks from his spot at our table. But honestly, I didn't care enough about Connor to ask him why he was acting so strangely. In fact, I cared so little for him that I'd always wondered why he'd never bothered to sit anywhere else, especially given that it should've been clear to him by now that none of the girls at our table were ever going to give him the time of day.

But I wasn't thinking about Connor at all that Wednesday. In fact, I went to Jake almost immediately once I entered the cafeteria, and pulled him aside to ask him for a ride to the LGBT resource center after school. It wasn't that I didn't think Sarah'd be willing to give me a ride, but given my reason for going, I decided it'd be best to just keep my trip from her altogether. If our positions were reversed and I knew my best friend and fake lesbian girlfriend was questioning her sexuality, I'd probably be understandably concerned. And I didn't want Sarah to be concerned. I just wanted her to land her guy and then we could start our fake breakup. Or I was pretty sure that was what I wanted.

Jake agreed to give me a ride, and mentioned needing to talk to Owen about our upcoming plans for October 11th anyway, so with that set, I spent the next few hours waiting for the day to end.

At last, three o'clock came. My last class was forced to stay a little late; it was lab day and we hadn't done a good enough job of cleaning up after ourselves, and we had one of those uptight teachers who insisted upon having everything spotless before anyone could leave the classroom.

I wound up fast-walking down a deserted hallway to my locker with the intention of meeting Jake by his car after I'd put my books away, but I paused right before I slammed my locker door shut, hearing familiar voices coming from within the boys' bathroom just across the hall.

"When? Next week?" one of the voices said.

Then came the other one: "Yeah, next Monday night. We've got a test in our English class we're gonna study for."

My eyebrows furrowed. That second voice was Sam, and the first boy sounded like one of the ones from the party. I heard laughter as I stood stock-still, my hand gripping my locker door tighter by the second.

"Man, you know you two won't be doing any studying, dyke girlfriend of hers or not." There was more laughter, and a sink came on.

"Yeah, probably not."

"Juggling two at once, though; that's gotta be tough for you to pull off. Christine'll be pissed if she finds out."

"So she won't. They don't talk, anyway."

"Ohhh… that's right. Although, maybe you could talk her into letting you have both. You know Sarah'd be up for it." As they laughed again, I was half-sure I'd squeezed a dent into the metal door between my fingers. My teeth were pressed together so tightly my mouth hurt.

"The perks of hooking up with a bi chick, dude."

The sink stopped running and I slammed the locker door so loudly it echoed up and down the hallway. Fuming, I rushed to get away from the bathroom, in no hurry to be caught by Sam and his asshole friend. It was no surprise to me that he was such a jerk, and the things he'd said about Sarah and me were infuriating.

But worst of all was that I wasn't sure Sarah would believe he'd said them.

I was quiet for most of the ride with Jake. The worst part about not being honest with anyone about Sarah and me was that when I *did* have a problem, I couldn't ask anyone for advice. As much as I wanted Jake's help, I couldn't tell him that Sarah was considering going on a study date with a boy who was only interested in using her.

Could I?

"So I saw something today," he said, toward the end of our drive. He seemed hesitant to share whatever it was with me, but eventually decided on continuing. "It might not even be a big deal, and I don't want you to think I'm on Jessa's side or anything with the whole confrontation between her and Sarah when you guys first joined LAMBDA... but I *did* see Sarah talking to Sam today."

I swallowed hard, not sure what to say to that. "Oh?"

"I think they made plans to hang out or something. It sounded like maybe next week they had a test to study for. I mean, that could be all it is... and if it makes a difference, he was definitely the one who seemed to be pushing it and initiated the conversation and everything, so Sarah could've just been trying to be nice. But I just thought you should know."

I was quiet for a moment. There were several ways to play this. I couldn't tell him the *whole* truth, but maybe I could tell him Sarah and I were on the rocks and that I was worried she was genuinely interested in Sam. And *then* I could tell him about what I'd heard in the bathroom and get his advice.

But I wasn't sure I was ready to toe the line like that yet. It was risky.

I swallowed hard, and said, at last, "Yeah, she told me about that, actually. It's totally cool."

"Oh, really? That's great." He looked a little embarrassed, and I felt my heart sink in my chest. "Sorry if I was being nosy or anything. I should've known she'd have already talked to you about it." He laughed suddenly, and shook his head. "Of course you guys have talked it all out. You're like the perfect couple."

"We are?" I raised an eyebrow disbelievingly.

He smiled over at me. "You don't think so? The rest of us envy the hell out of you. Two pretty, popular girls... we all dream of being part of something like that."

"Well... we have our ups and downs just like everyone else," I mumbled.

He just laughed again, and soon enough, we were at the resource center and walking into the lobby. Owen was there at the front desk, and he greeted us with a grin. "Hey, guys! Here to talk about Sunday? I was thinking we'd all meet here about noon, and then set up what we need to for Monday the 11th."

"That sounds great," Jake agreed, and turned to me abruptly. "That was what I was here to talk about. What were you doing here again, Katie?"

"Oh. Um..." I looked around quickly and spotted the bookshelf across the room. "I've been meaning to finish up the first season of *The L Word*, and I thought you guys might have the box set?"

"Of course. We have every season," Owen told me. "Feel free to go check out the bookshelf and grab whatever you'd like."

"Cool."

I left Owen and Jake to talk, and made my way over to the shelves, scanning them uncomfortably. Every now and then, I glanced over my shoulder, wondering how on earth I was supposed to get Owen alone.

And then my eyes landed on a book on the bottom row of the shelf: *How Do I Know? The LGBT Guide for Questioning Teens*.

I glanced over my shoulder again, and then hastily grabbed the book and opened it to the table of contents. There was a chapter on childhood

144

signs, a chapter on coming out, a chapter on accepting yourself...

I snapped the book shut when I felt a tap on my shoulder, and spun around to see Owen standing there. He raised both eyebrows at me, reacting to how jumpy I was. Jake was now across the room, flipping through the same magazine Violet had been reading just yesterday.

"Hey, sorry about that," Owen laughed out. "How are you doing?"

"Oh, fine." I tried to hide the book title, but he caught a glimpse of it anyway.

"For questioning teens," he echoed. "You seem a little bit past that, judging from what I saw of you yesterday."

I glanced over at Jake again, surprised to feel my cheeks growing warm. "Um," I finally mumbled, "is there somewhere we could talk alone?"

"Sure," he agreed, nodding. "I've got an office just this way." He pointed down a nearby hallway, and I caught Jake's attention as Owen and I left the lobby, gesturing to him that I'd be right back. He looked curious, but nodded.

Owen closed the door behind us once we were alone in his office, and we took a seat in two chairs with a desk between us. "Is everything alright?" he asked me.

I realized pretty quickly that this conversation was going to be a tough one. His first question already felt loaded. "Things are... complicated," I finally said.

"Well, that's what we're here for," he told me. "Ask away, or say whatever you'd like. I'm an open book and I'm all ears."

I swallowed hard, my gaze falling to the book still gripped in my hands. Finally, I asked him, "I guess I was wondering... How did you know you were gay?"

He didn't answer at first, and I raised my eyes to him hastily.

"Wait, you *are* gay, right?"

He laughed at that. "Yes, I am." He sat back in his chair and rubbed at his chin thoughtfully. "I believe I was... hmm. Right around your age, actually. Maybe a couple years younger, at most. And I knew because I fell in love with a boy at my school."

"How'd you know you were in love?" I asked.

"Well, that's a question I can't answer," he admitted. "When you feel it, you just know."

"But does that mean that everyone who isn't sure if they feel it isn't in love?"

"Not necessarily. Feelings are confusing. There are thousands of books written about one feeling, and all of them say thousands of different and sometimes contradictory things."

"So you're saying you can't help me," I said.

He smiled at me. "Well, what is it you need help with?"

I chewed on my lower lip. I couldn't tell *Jake* my whole story; he'd probably hate me. But Owen's job was to not judge. Still, being honest was always risky.

At last, I took a deep breath, and admitted, "I kind of did something terrible."

He looked curious, now. "What makes you say that?"

"Because it's the truth." I swallowed a lump in my throat, and continued, "My friend and I, Sarah... you met her yesterday. We're best friends, and about a month ago, Jake mistook us for a couple. So ever since then, we've pretended to be one. We haven't told anyone else the truth."

I didn't dare look at Owen, but I heard him shift in his seat. Finally, he asked me, "What made you want to pretend to be a couple?"

"I didn't want to, but it wasn't up to me. It happened really fast and Sarah just kind of said we were. She wanted attention from this dumb guy."

"So she thought being into girls would make her more appealing," Owen guessed. I nodded.

"I knew it was a bad idea, but I couldn't go back on it once it'd been done, because everyone was really happy to have two new people they could relate to. I didn't want to disappoint them. I didn't want people to hate us. But now it's been a month and things have gotten... weird. Not to mention this guy she likes is a complete asshole, and I know she's just going to end up getting hurt but I don't know what to do about it."

"Well, have you tried talking to her?" he suggested.

"I don't know what that'll do. She probably wouldn't even believe he said the things he did, anyway."

"I don't mean about the guy," Owen corrected. "I mean about how you feel."

I let out a bitter laugh. "No way. I don't even know how I feel. Why else would I be here? Besides, I seriously doubt she'd give up on a guy she's been crushing on for four years to be with a girl, even if that *was* what I wanted. Which it definitely isn't, so." I folded my arms across my chest defensively, watching him with a sharp gaze.

"What's wrong with wanting that? Are you worried about being rejected?" he asked me.

I forced a laugh. "Uh, I've seen enough movies to know what happens when you fall for your straight best friend. I can like girls; that's fine, but I don't want to get my heart broken. I'd like to like someone who will like me back, you know?"

Owen tapped at his chin for another long moment. "So from my understanding, you started out faking being gay, and now you're saying you don't like your friend, but you're still worried you might actually be gay for other, potentially related reasons," he recapped. It felt strange to have it said aloud. Like he was talking about someone else I was watching from afar. Someone who wasn't me.

"I don't know," I said at last. "I'm not sure I should even think about it. Maybe if I didn't, I'd stop being so confused and all of this would just go away. Then things could eventually get back to normal."

"Do your parents know what you're going through?"

"They're the ones putting me through it!" I told him, exasperated. "Everything was fine, or at least it was okay, but then they had to go and actually *believe* I was gay, and I didn't have it in me to tell them the whole thing with Sarah was staged, so I had to just sit there and listen to them tell me about how they'd always known and how they just wanted me to be myself."

"You're very fortunate to have parents like that," he said.

"Yeah, but I'd have preferred ones that didn't tell me I've always been gay when I'm not sure how I feel about anything or anyone anymore. Things were a lot less confusing when I hadn't kissed any girls."

"You've kissed Sarah," he guessed.

"And another girl," I mumbled. Both of his eyebrows shot up, and he looked genuinely thrown for a loop.

"*Really*? Multiple girls?" Then he paused, amused. "So I see. Between that and the response from your parents, you've built a quite a good case for liking girls."

"Exactly. So how do I know for sure whether I do or not?" I watched him expectantly, eager to hear his answer.

He shrugged his shoulders. "I can't tell you, to be perfectly honest. All I can say is that you have to answer that for yourself. Look inside your heart."

I sank back in my seat and deadpanned, "Seriously? That's all you've got?"

He gave me a sympathetic smile. "Katie, I know it seems like I haven't helped, but nobody else can tell you whether you're gay or not. Not even your parents. I can tell you how *I* knew, and you can read all of the books you want, but the answer is something only you can give to yourself. Do you like how you feel when you're with Sarah? Do you like kissing girls? How about boys? And most importantly: Do you really want to spend hours on end worrying about a label right now? I've found that my life got a whole lot easier when I stopped thinking so much and just started *feeling*. That was how I got my answer."

Owen took a breath, and continued, "My suggestion is that you go with the flow. You're already facing the negative consequences of being openly gay, so the upside is that you have a lot less to lose than most questioning teens. It's a small comfort, but a comfort nonetheless. So that's my advice. Stop thinking and let yourself feel." He got to his feet, and that was my cue that we were done.

"And hey, listen," he added as he moved to open the door to his office, "what I *can* be sure of is that gay, bisexual, straight, asexual, pansexual, *whatever* you are... you will always be welcome here."

"Thank you," I said. As unresolved as my issues felt, his words were still oddly comforting.

"And please, *please* be honest with your friends, when you can be," he added. "It won't be easy, but it's the right thing to do."

And then we were out of his office and heading back to Jake, and I was still confused, but strangely, *thankfully*, being confused felt *okay*.

At least for now.

Chapter Nine

"So I heard about you and Sam. Monday night, right?"

Sarah looked up from her spot across from me on her bedroom floor. She was halfway through painting the toenails of her right foot a dark blue-green color, and a Calculus book sat open beside her. It was Friday, and I'd given her two days to tell me about Sam herself. Now it was clear she simply hadn't planned on sharing. I wasn't sure what that meant.

"Uh, yeah." She went back to her toenails, sounding distracted. "He asked me to study."

"You know he's not actually interested in studying, right?"

"Of course." She arched an eyebrow at me, pausing again. "Wasn't that the plan all along?"

"I guess." I shrugged my shoulders and looked away from her. My mind felt scattered, and I noticed another book – the one she'd checked out from the resource center earlier in the week – lying on her bedroom floor, just a few feet away. The bookmark stuck inside of it told me she didn't have long to go before she was finished with it.

"You don't sound very convinced," she observed.

"I just..." I trailed off, then took a deep breath. "Um, wasn't there some other girl he was flirting with? The one from the party?"

"Yeah, Christine. I texted him; asked him about it. He said they're not serious."

"What if he's lying?"

She laughed and shook her head, eyes still on her toes as she painted them. "Why would he lie?"

"Because jock assholes kind of do that?"

She pursed her lips together as she finished with the nail polish, then closed the bottle and set it aside. Her eyes snapped to mine, then, and she tilted her head to the side. "I didn't know my spending an evening with a guy I've liked since freshman year would be such a problem."

"It's not," I retorted instinctively. "I just think you should be careful."

"Well, thank you for caring," she replied, sounding not very thankful at all. I shifted uncomfortably. This was going about as well as I'd expected it would.

"Look, Sarah. All I'm saying is that there are guys out there who don't respect girls. I'd hate for you to get hurt."

"You know, that's funny, because last week you said it was *great* that I was getting attention from him. Now all of a sudden it's not a good idea? I'm kind of getting mixed signals here, Katie." She got to her feet and crossed the room to her desk, putting her nail polish away.

"You're pissed," I realized, sighing deeply.

"I'm not," she countered. "Just frustrated." She rejoined me on the floor with a sigh of her own, and her eyes met mine. She didn't look away, and I felt strangely exposed as she told me, "Katie, I get that things have been weird lately. I've thought about it a lot, and I get all of it. If you don't want me to hang out with Sam, you can just say so."

I swallowed the lump in my throat, and told her, quietly, "I don't want you to hang out with Sam."

Her eyes didn't leave mine. "Okay. Why not?" she asked.

I swallowed again. This time, the lump didn't go away. "I... um." I paused, closed my eyes, and then avoided her gaze as I told her, "I just don't think he's a good guy."

She didn't really react, beyond a sigh I was half-sure I imagined, and then she was reaching for the

Calculus book on the floor and pulling it onto her lap.

"I need to study, so let me know when you want me to take you home," was all she said, and I felt confident in that moment that the lump in my throat would be there forever.

Sunday, LAMBDA met Owen at the resource center as planned, and I kept my distance from both Owen and Sarah. She sensed I wasn't very eager to talk to her, and spent most of the day with Hattie and Henry, cutting out circular stickers and printing out fliers that advertised National Coming Out Day, while I found myself hanging out with Violet and Jake, making banners to hang around the school. That was Jake's plan: to decorate the halls and walls and lockers early Monday morning. I wasn't sure how well-received his idea would be come Monday, but it seemed well-intentioned enough, and so I was excited to finally start paying my dues to the people I'd felt like I'd been using for the past month.

"If we can make even one more person at our school feel like they have a safe environment if they want to come out, we've done our jobs," Jake declared to the rest of the group at the end of the day, when we'd finally finished the decorations. "Now all we have to do is get a few volunteers to come to school early tomorrow morning and stick this stuff up everywhere, and our work here is done."

Owen gave us a round of applause, and we all joined in, sweaty but grinning. I had one banner I was particularly proud of; I wasn't a great artist, but I'd managed to paint a pretty massive rainbow flag onto it, and both Violet and Jake had complimented me on it.

As we all filed out of the building, Jake nudged me and asked, "Are you gonna help Monday morning? We've got a lot of stuff to put up."

"Sure," I agreed. "I'll be there, if you'll give me a ride."

And I was. Monday morning, most of us came to school early. Jake and I were the first ones there, and we got started on the main hallway. My rainbow flag banner went up first, and Jake taped several fliers to the walls and put one small sticker in every locker. When everyone else from the club finally showed up, he handed out stacks of the stickers and delegated us to different parts of the school, so that every locker would get one.

Sarah, to my surprise, showed up as well, but it was Hattie who wound up assigned to the same hallway as me, and as we walked along opposite ends, I asked her, "Do you think this sticker thing's a good idea? I mean, what if people don't want them?"

"It's just a sticker," she laughed out. "People are ignorant, but I can't imagine anyone'd make that big a deal out of it. Would you get mad if the chess club left a sticker advertising National Chess Day in your locker?"

"No," I admitted. "Maybe I'm just paranoid."

An hour later, at seven thirty, students began piling into the school by the dozens. I went to my first class, which started at eight, and honestly, I didn't think much more about the whole National Coming Out Day thing.

I met Sarah by my locker after class, just off of the main hallway, and we played nice for the students who still wasted their time staring at us, despite the fact that things were still a little tense between us. Once I'd gotten my books for my next couple of classes, I moved in the direction of my next period, toward the main hallway. Sarah grabbed my arm quickly.

"Hey, do you mind if we detour? I need to refill my water bottle."

"You fill it up every morning," I dismissed. "Shouldn't you have plenty left?"

"Yeah, but I need more," she replied weakly. I rolled my eyes at her, a little suspicious, and continued toward the main hallway. She fell into step beside me, fidgeting.

"What's up with you?" I asked her.

"Nothing. I just... really think we should go a different way."

"Why?"

She bit her lip and didn't answer, and a moment later, I found out why.

In the main hallway, the banner I'd worked hard on now rested on the floor, torn into several pieces and sporting dozens of dusty footprints. Even as I stared, several more students walked right over what remained of it. I took it in with furrowed eyebrows, my throat tightening.

"Cool," I mumbled at last, and hurried on to the next hallway, Sarah barely keeping up with me.

"It was probably Brett Larson and the other asshole football players," she told me. "You know he's had it out for you since that day you stood up to him."

"Other asshole football players. Like your boyfriend?" I shot back.

"He's not my boyfriend yet," she countered.

"Well, I'm sure you two will be very happy together after tonight."

"That's really not fair of you to say after-" she started to say, but before she could finish, Connor suddenly appeared in front of us, his eyebrows pulled together anxiously. Both Sarah and I stopped in the hallway, staring at him, but his eyes were only on me.

"Hey, Katie. Uh..." He glanced to Sarah at last, looking nervous, and, when he realized she wasn't going anywhere, simply lowered his voice and asked, "I was kind of wondering if you would come over to my house after school? Just to talk and stuff."

I saw Sarah tense beside me out of my peripheral vision, and my response was completely instinctive; a dumb, heat-of-the-moment decision.

"Yeah, sure. I'd love to," I told him. He looked surprised by my answer, and gave me a small smile. It was unlike him, but it suited him better than his usual cocky grin.

"Really? Awesome. See you then. And at lunch, but... yeah." He nodded once and then left us alone, and Sarah glared at me when he was gone.

"Seriously?"

"What? You're the only one who can spend an afternoon with a guy?"

"That's really clever, Katie," she snapped, and left without waiting for a response.

I watched her storm away, my eyebrows furrowed, and then, right around the time she was turning a corner and disappearing from my sight, I realized what I'd just agreed to. I wasn't remotely attracted to Connor, and now I'd agreed to go to his house. It really was an awful idea. But at the same time, there was something satisfying about knowing that it bothered Sarah.

I got through lunch and a couple of classes with Sarah easily enough. We ignored each other, and weren't so great at hiding that we were ignoring each other, which left everyone involved in our personal lives aware of the fact that we were upset with each other. That situation had been awkward enough back when we were just friends, but now that we were pretending to be a couple, it was even more uncomfortable.

By the end of the day, I wanted to tell Connor that I'd changed my mind about going home with him, but as we walked out to his car together, I saw Sarah joining Sam in *his* car, and that strengthened my resolve. Even if I didn't actually do anything with Connor, there were some upsides to letting Sarah *think* I had.

I think Sarah expected me to chicken out, too, because as I passed her and Sam and climbed into Connor's jeep, I saw her look directly at me, her eyebrows furrowed and her mouth turned down into a frown. But then Sam said something to her and her attention was on him, and Connor was starting his jeep and telling me, "Thanks for coming with me. I kind of thought you'd say no for sure."

"Yeah, well... you asked nicely. I'm not used to that from you," I admitted.

"Yeah," he echoed. "I know I've been kind of an ass."

"You say that like you're done being an ass," I said.

"Maybe I am," he replied.

We reached his house within minutes, and I felt my trepidation grow when I realized there were no other cars in the driveway or in the garage. His parents weren't home.

"I guess the basement's as good a place as any," he suggested once we were inside. He opened a door to reveal a set of stairs that curled into the darkness, and when he saw my hesitation, he insisted, "I just wanna talk. I swear."

"Would you blame me for not really trusting you?" I asked him, moving away from him when he offered me his hand.

"Not at all. But I'm asking you to," he replied. I studied him. There was something different about him. Gone was the arrogant asshole I'd known for a couple of years now. Instead, Connor seemed anxious. Nervous. And he was staring at me pleadingly, which was certainly not a look I'd ever seen on him before.

I sighed and took his hand. "Okay. But if you murder me, Sarah knows I'm here."

He laughed as he led me down the stairs. "Damn. And here I thought I was going to get away with it."

We reached the basement, and he turned a light on. I was pleasantly surprised. The room was finished, with a carpet and a couch and several video game stations that rested on a large cabinet alongside a television. "This is kind of cool," I admitted.

"Right?" he agreed. "My parents had it put in for my brothers and me when we moved in."

"I didn't know you had brothers." I took a seat beside him on the couch and folded my hands in my lap. I considered, for the first time, that I was supposed to be dating Sarah, and yet Connor had invited me here anyway. He wasn't acting like a jerk, but it certainly seemed like his goal was to try and "turn me straight", or whatever it was guys like him thought they were doing when they hooked up with girls who called themselves lesbians.

"Three older ones," he confirmed, and then cleared his throat abruptly. "Anyway... so here we are."

"Here we are," I echoed, growing uncomfortable again.

"Um..." He took a deep breath, and when I looked over at him, I noticed that he was trembling slightly. "Look, I really am glad you came, especially because I know it pissed Sarah off and caused trouble for you guys. I didn't know who else to talk to. I've never done anything like this before, and I guess... you were so nice at the party when I was upset, and I get that you don't remember most of it because if you did you wouldn't look so confused right now." He forced a laugh, and I blinked at him, clueless. I had absolutely no idea what he was talking about.

"Wait... what happened at the party?"

"Some guy just pissed me off. Made a stupid comment." He shook my question off. "I guess, uh... what I'm trying to say is that I thought today would be a good day..." He clenched his teeth together and his arms shook. I put a hand on his shoulder to try and still him; seeing him this scared was starting to scare *me*.

"Connor?"

He let out another deep breath, and laughed a little. "I don't know why this is so hard; you're gonna be totally cool with it, obviously, but, ah..." He paused, working himself up, and then announced, "I'm kind of bisexual."

I stared at him. I was sure I hadn't heard him right.

He let out a long rush of air, like he'd been holding it all in for minutes, and then slouched back against the couch, putting both hands on top of his head. "Wow. I think that's the first time I've ever even said it aloud."

"*You're* bisexual," I repeated, hardly daring to believe it. Connor, *asshole* Connor, Connor who'd contributed to the dozens of terrible comments sent Sarah and my way over the course of the past five weeks... *that* Connor liked guys?

"What a way to celebrate National Coming Out Day. Here I am," he said, nodding at me. "Man, I've been keeping that in for what, a year and a half now?"

"Are you being serious right now?" I asked him. "Like, you're really bisexual?"

"Yeah." He nodded again. "I guess that's kind of why I'm an ass. I thought I could just be, you know, one of the guys and no one would know."

"And you were right," I marveled, blinking up at him. "Wow."

"I think I, uh, actually kind of prefer guys," he admitted shyly. "But girls are hot too. I just wanted to tell someone, and I thought you'd understand, between our talk at the party and you being gay and all. You won't tell anyone, right? I'm gonna be better now. I never meant any of the stuff I said to you and Sarah, and I'll leave you guys alone now. I'll leave Hannah alone. I just kind of wanna finish high school and get out of here, you know?"

"Yeah," I agreed quietly. "Don't worry, Connor. I won't tell anyone." And I wouldn't, although it would be pretty damn tempting. But I wouldn't wish what I'd gone through on anyone. Not even Connor.

"Alright. Thanks." He hesitated, and then told me, "Well, I might still have to be an ass sometimes. Just to, you know, fit in. But now you'll know it's an act. That's an improvement, right?"

I just sighed at him. *There* was the Connor I was used to.

In the distance, his doorbell rang, and we both looked to the stairs that led to the front door, confused. "Are you expecting company?" I asked, though his expression was an answer in itself.

"Nah. Wonder who it is?"

We both made our way back upstairs, and Connor went ahead of me, reaching the door first as I hung back by his kitchen counter. I saw a flash of brunette hair through the translucent glass of the door, and then Connor was opening it and I was staring at the doorway in surprise.

"Sarah?" Connor and I asked at the same time, and she immediately pushed past Connor, her gaze steely as she headed straight for me.

"Are you okay?" she asked me abruptly, and I nodded dumbly at her, baffled as to what she was doing here. She was supposed to be with Sam.

"Good." She rounded on Connor, who immediately looked afraid for his life. "Listen, asshole. If you so much as touched her, you're gonna be jealous of what Ken dolls have between their legs."

"We were just talking," Connor told her, his face reddening. "I swear. I didn't know when I asked that her coming over here would be such a big problem."

"Well, now you do. Stay away from my girlfriend." She reached for my hand, and then I was being led out of Connor's house and out to Sarah's car. Part of me was completely confused as to what was going on and was kind of interested in hearing more from Connor about how he came to the conclusion that he was bisexual... but another part of me was kind of just mostly marveling at how angry Sarah was. I'd never really seen her this mad before.

"What were you thinking?" she hissed at me when we were safely in her car. "*Connor?*"

"You didn't seem to have such a massive problem with it earlier today," I pointed out.

"Because I didn't think you'd actually be crazy enough to go through with it! He's so sleazy, Katie."

"He was nice," I told her. "You didn't have to come get me. Weren't you supposed to spend today with Sam?"

"Yeah, well..." She sucked in a breath and moved to pull out of Connor's driveway. "That lasted all of five minutes before I told him to take me back to the school."

"And then you came here," I said. She didn't reply. "What about Sam?"

"I don't know, Katie," she sighed out. "Things are little..." she trailed off, and just kind of shook her head and made a confused motion with her hand before finishing, "right now."

I sat back in my seat, not sure what to say to that. But Sarah wasn't done talking. She let out an exasperated groan, and said, "God, why can't you just...? I don't know."

"You're not making much sense," I admitted.

"That makes two of us," she mumbled. I glanced at her to see she was staring straight ahead, her hands tight on the steering wheel.

"Thanks for saving me," I said at last. I didn't want to blow Connor's secret, and I assumed he'd prefer Sarah hating him to her knowing the truth. At least for now.

"You're welcome. I seriously don't even know what you were thinking."

I turned away from her to look out my window. "I was thinking that you weren't the only one who deserved attention from a guy."

"God, since when does that shit matter to you?" she countered. "You're above that, Katie. C'mon."

"You don't practice what you preach," I observed.

"Yeah, but that's just how I am. That's what makes you a better person than me."

I closed my eyes and leaned back, resting my head on the seat. I sighed. "Can't you just stay away from Sam?" I felt the bump of the curb as we pulled up into my driveway, and Sarah stopped the car and put it into park.

"Why?"

"Are you gonna ask me that every time?"

"Yes."

I opened my eyes and looked over at her. "I heard him saying he didn't care that we were together. He wanted to hook up with you anyway, and he wanted to lie to you and that other girl – Christine – from the party. Like, juggle both of you at the same time. He doesn't care about you, Sarah. He doesn't want a relationship. He's just a liar."

She took that in with her eyes in her lap, and I pressed on.

"I know you might not believe me, but I wouldn't lie about this, okay?"

"You wouldn't," she agreed, much to my surprise. "You're a good person." She raised her gaze to meet mine, and offered me a small, forced smile. "Which is why you don't deserve someone like Connor. But maybe I go well with someone like Sam."

"Don't be stupid," I murmured.

"It's not." She reached over and unlocked the car doors. Her silent signal that she was ready for me to get out. "Katie, do you know what people say about me?"

"What, that you're smart?" I guessed. "That you're pretty and popular?"

She forced a laugh. "Not exactly."

"Then what?"

"That I sleep around with a lot of guys." She looked away from me, and the silence that followed her statement ate at my chest. I chewed at the inside of my cheek. "That I'm a slut, a skank... that I use people. That I need to pick a side, that I should stop whoring myself out, that I must be a freak in bed, that I can't *possibly* have a brain and must only be getting good grades because I'm screwing teachers. And most of that stuff was said before this whole thing started with us, but it's only gotten worse since." She shook her head. "So I guess maybe there was a part of me that knew what Sam was like all along and just realized we'd be a good fit. A guy who doesn't want to settle down and a girl no one believes *can*."

I wanted to tell her, right then in her car, that she wasn't any of those things. Every word was on the tip of my tongue, and I knew how to comfort her if I'd chosen to. I'd say that she wasn't a slut just because she wasn't a virgin, and I'd point out that I wasn't a virgin either. I'd tell her that teenagers are shallow and judgmental and that most of our peers were too stupid to look beneath the surface and realize she was more than just her looks. I'd tell her any guy would be lucky to be with her, not the other way around, and I'd tell her she was smart and funny and kind and that I loved everything about her; that she was the one flawed person I thought was perfect anyway.

But I was awkward and scared and confused and lacking the confidence to say any of those things to even my own best friend – the girl I should've trusted most to accept them from me – and so I didn't.

I didn't, and she was back in Sam's car the next afternoon.

Chapter Ten

After that day, Sarah and I made up publicly. We'd perfected it by now, the art of acting like a happy couple no matter how complicated things were behind the scenes, but it helped that a day after our conversation in Sarah's car, I opened my locker to dozens of National Coming Out Day stickers that'd been modified with sharpie to say, rather uncleverly, "National Dyke Day". Brett Larson didn't hide the fact that they were from him; there was also a little folded note that simply had a smiley face drawn on it with his signature at the bottom.

Sarah helped me throw all of the stickers away, and then, in a show of confidence meant to dissuade Brett and any of our other classmates from trying anything else, she kissed me at my locker for so long that I wound up with day-long butterflies.

I knew, after that, that if I didn't find a way to change things, I'd wind up being the loser girl who fell for her straight best friend. And I did not want to be that girl. I'd watched over half a season of *The L Word* and a couple of gay movies by then; I knew what happened to that girl. She wound up sad and rejected, and then – only if she was lucky – with an eventual new love interest who was *actually* into girls.

So I tried to put Sarah from my mind, as hard as that was given that I saw her on a daily basis, and I let her keep doing whatever it was she was doing with Sam. And I was perfectly content to stay ignorant about whatever that was.

She missed a club meeting two weeks later to hang out with him, and Jake announced his next new project to us that day.

"The Winter Formal's coming up in about five weeks, and Principal Crenshaw just released the ticket prices. Twenty dollars per person, or thirty for a couple." He paused. "Couples, however, are restricted to a heterosexual definition."

"Are you serious?" Hattie asked. "That's so not fair!"

"I've already tried to talk him into changing his mind. I spoke with him today," Jake said. "But he said that he doesn't want to leave the opportunity for friends to say they're a couple just to save money."

"But what about girls and guys who are just friends?" Henry cut in.

"Well, exactly. Obviously it's a double-standard. But I thought of a way to show him we won't let him forget that real gay couples do exist at this school and deserve to be treated the same as the rest of the students here." He paused again, this time for dramatic effect, and then declared, "We're going to get a gay couple nominated for Winter Formal King and Queen. Or should I say: Queen and Queen."

And then, abruptly, everyone's eyes were on me. I looked around at them all, baffled. "Wait... me and Sarah?"

"Do you see any of the rest of us winning?" Jessa asked, raising an eyebrow. She had a point, but I still wasn't as confident as Jake seemed to be.

"I don't think we could win, either," I admitted. "Who would vote for us?"

"Everyone gay, tons of gay-friendly students, and you'd also get the prankster vote and the vote of anyone who just doesn't want the same old jocks and cheerleaders winning it," Jake pointed out. "You two would basically sweep the 'other' vote, *and* you'd get votes from your social circles and your supporters."

"Supporters," I echoed, feeling overwhelmed. "Okay?"

"I want to get started on campaigning as soon as possible," Jake declared. "Nominations are in two weeks. Principal Crenshaw will try to put a lid on this, I'm sure, but he can't ignore hundreds of nominations."

"He could," Violet pointed out. "So we have to not let him."

"Exactly," Jake agreed. "So let's make this happen, guys. Let's show them that just because they ignore us doesn't mean we'll go away."

"So what'd I miss today?"

I put my phone on speaker, and set it down on my bathroom counter as I straightened my hair.

"They're trying to get us nominated for King and Queen at the Winter Formal."

Sarah let out a light laugh. "Really?"

"Really."

"How do they plan on doing that? I thought only straight couples could be nominated."

"Well, that's obviously not very fair, so they're gonna fight it and see how it goes."

"Huh. That sounds kind of cool. We'd look cute in our little crowns up on stage."

"Yep." I ran a few strands of my hair through the straightener and watched steam rise toward the bathroom ceiling.

"What are you doing?" Sarah asked. "I keep hearing a weird noise."

"I'm straightening my hair," I told her.

"Why? You don't have a date, do you?"

"I don't see why I'd have to tell you if I did."

On the other end, she let out a heavy sigh. "Wow, we almost went two whole minutes without getting snippy. A new record."

"I wasn't being snippy, Sarah. I'm just saying. I don't ask about you and Sam; you don't ask about my love life. I thought that was what we were doing."

"I can't ask as your best friend and not as your girlfriend?"

"In case you haven't noticed, it's been a little hard to tell the difference lately."

She was quiet for a moment. And then she sounded a little defeated as she replied, "Okay, fine. Bye." She hung up the phone and my throat tightened. I felt tears pricking at the corners of my eyes and hastily wiped them away.

When I was finished with my hair and I'd spent a few minutes staring at my glassy-eyed reflection in the mirror, I went downstairs to meet with my parents, who were already ready to go. They shared a smile as I descended the stairs, and my father offered me his hand. "You look gorgeous tonight, Madame."

"Shut up, Dad," I said, forcing a laugh and smacking his arm. Mom grinned at the both of us as we walked out to the car.

It was a tri-monthly tradition of ours to go out to a nice family dinner together. Like, a really *nice* dinner, with several courses and waiters in tuxedos. We weren't as well-off financially as Sarah's family, but we held our own, and this was a luxury we could afford four times a year.

We had reservations at the restaurant, so we were seated right away, and as Mom and Dad ordered appetizers, I looked around at the other patrons. Most of them were couples, and all of the couples were straight. I noted the latter fact almost subconsciously, and then wondered when I'd started paying attention to the fact that everyone around me was straight. Was that a side-effect of questioning one's sexuality?

Mom went to use the bathroom right around the time we were being brought our drinks, and Dad cleared his throat, setting his appetizer aside for a moment and telling me, "So I was thinking for your next birthday that your Mom and I should repaint your room for you. I know you've always hated the color."

"Really?" I asked, sitting up straighter in my seat.

"Yeah. We were thinking a mix of six colors. Just a giant rainbow across all four walls."

"Jerk," I shot back, throwing my napkin at him as he chuckled. "You got my hopes up just to make a gay joke."

"And it was worth it," he declared. "Anyway, I haven't seen any girls over lately. Not even Sarah. Your mom's gonna want grandchildren, you know."

"Dad," I whined, pulling a face. "We are seriously not having this conversation right now."

"What about Sarah?" Mom cut in, retaking her seat on my other side. "I heard her name."

"I was just asking Katie if they were gonna give us grandchildren."

I pressed my hand to my face as Mom shot Dad a disappointed look. "I hate to break it to you, Jeff, but I don't think that's how procreation works."

"I hear they're working on the technology for it, now," Dad pointed out.

"God, I am *not* having kids with Sarah," I sighed out, eager to change the subject. "We're not even really talking much right now."

"Why not?" Mom asked, jumping on that immediately. I was grateful; anything beat grandkids.

"Because she's still hung up on that guy, even after I told her he was using her. I heard him say he wanted to try and juggle Sarah and this other girl he likes, but she just said maybe they were a good match anyway." I shrugged my shoulders, my mood dampening. Maybe this wasn't such a good topic of conversation after all. "Anyway, that was about two weeks ago, and I haven't heard much from her about it since then, but I haven't really been asking."

Mom and Dad exchanged looks, and then Mom put down her silverware and moved her hand to place it over mine on the table. "Katie, you have to remember that Sarah has had a very different upbringing from you."

"What does that have anything to do with this?" I asked.

"Well, she doesn't have the same relationship with her parents that you do," Mom elaborated. "You've had your tough moments growing up, sure, but do you remember when you were struggling with self-esteem issues in middle school and you had your father and me there to support you? Imagine if you hadn't had us. That's what life is like for Sarah."

"But Sarah has *us*," I reminded them. "We're like her second family."

"It's not the same, honey. I wish it were. I wish she was over at our house constantly rather than being holed up alone in hers, but sometimes you just can't make someone stay for dinner." She hesitated, and then continued, "Sarah has always been a very driven girl, and I think that comes from having parents who could only be impressed when she was really, *really* impressive. And sure, having parents you feel like you need to impress by getting A's might make you get A's, but it can also make you feel like if you *don't* get A's, you aren't good enough. And I think there are probably a lot of times when Sarah didn't feel good enough."

I had no idea what to say to that. Sarah always seemed so carefree. She was always having fun, and she'd always seemed to *like* not having her parents around. I'd never really seriously considered the downsides. "But she's still a good person," I said, getting a little defensive, and Mom nodded her agreement.

"Of course she is. But I'm not so sure *she* knows that."

Violet tapped me on my shoulder at my locker the next day, and when I turned around, she had a stack of fliers in her hands and was grinning widely at me.

"I have news from Jake," she said. "About the Winter Formal."

"Okay. What's up?"

"So Principal Crenshaw found out we wanted to get you guys nominated, and he totally panicked and pulled the 'straight couples only' rule from the ticket pricings. Which means gay couples like you and Sarah can get in for the discount."

"That's fantastic," I told her, genuinely surprised. "Awesome!"

"It gets better. He did it so that we'd back off on the whole 'Queen and Queen' plan. Only we're not going to." She smirked. "And there's nothing he can do about it unless he wants to blatantly discriminate against gay people and deal with us raising a big stink over it. So not only did we get the discount... we're gonna help you guys snag the crowns, too."

She offered me one of the fliers in her hands, and I stared down at it for a moment, not quite sure what I was looking at at first. Then, slowly, I smiled, and glanced back up at her. "Wait... this is Sarah and me."

"Yeah." She looked down at one of the fliers still in her hands, and I stared at the one she'd given me. There were two pictures at the top of the flier, one above the other. The first was one that'd been taken of us in elementary school, when we were both tiny and gap-toothed. I remembered it; we were at Six Flags and Sarah had a giant stuffed animal in one of her hands. Her other hand gripped mine, and we were both smiling so widely I was surprised we weren't in pain.

Beneath that photo was a second, much more recent one that'd been taken by Hannah using

Sarah's cell phone at lunch, right around the time we'd started pretending to date. My cheeks were flushed but I was smiling, and Sarah was right beside me, her cheek pressed to mine and a matching smile on her face. Beneath the photos was a statement encouraging people to nominate us.

"Where did you get those pictures?" I asked eventually, looking up at Violet.

"Sarah," she said. "Aren't they adorable?"

"Sarah gave you these?"

"Yeah. She said they were her favorites." She grinned at me, almost conspiratorially.

Then, without any warning, we suddenly had company in the form of Christine Goddard, and Violet was struggling to press the fliers to her own chest even as Christine shot us both *and* the fliers a condescending look all at once.

"Cute," she deadpanned, and her eyes snapped to me. "Hi. Katie, right? I have an important message I need you to deliver, okay?" She didn't wait for a response before continuing, "Tell your little girlfriend to stay the hell away from *my* boyfriend."

"Boyfriend?" I asked dumbly. When had *that* happened?

"That's right." She smirked. "As of last week, Sam and I are dating, and last time I checked, Sarah was supposed to be with *you*, so there's really no reason I should be finding her driver's license in Sam's car." She retrieved the card in question and shoved it into my hands. I glanced down at it, inwardly groaning. It was, in fact, Sarah's. "Oh, and by the way... don't even bother running for King and Queen, or Queen and Queen, or whatever. Because Sam and I are going to win."

She stalked off without another word, and I wrinkled my nose as I watched her go. "Well, I guess we definitely can't run now," I told Violet. "Not since Queen Christine told me not to."

"What was Sarah doing in Sam Heath's car?" she asked me, looking slightly amused.

"They have a class together," I answered. "They've got a study group going. Christine's just paranoid."

"*You* seem fine," Violet observed. "Although I guess with pictures like these, there's not really any reason to doubt your relationship." She tapped the fliers and smiled at me. "Anyway, gotta go to class. I'll see you around."

"Bye."

Violet left, and I stared down at Sarah's drivers' license, then let out a sigh and stuffed it into my pants pocket with a shake of my head. I wasn't even sure I wanted to know what she was getting herself into at this point, but, knowing Sarah, it was going to be messy.

I presented Sarah with her license near the end of lunch, and she was surprised to see I had it. "Where'd you find this? I've been missing it for, like, two days now."

"I'll tell you later," I mumbled. In the midst of our friends wasn't exactly the best place to bring up Sam.

"Oh, so I forgot to mention: I've been seeing fliers everywhere today," Dina announced, shooting Sarah and me a knowing look. "You guys didn't tell us you were running for Winter Formal Queens."

"It's more Jake pushing it than anything," I admitted. "You know, to make a statement."

"Well, *I'm* voting to nominate the two of you, if it's any consolation," Graham cut in. "Better you guys than the same old popular kids. No offense, Hannah."

"Don't worry; I hope they win, too," Hannah agreed, smiling. "Christine deserves to be dethroned for once. I hear she's running with Sam Heath."

"Yeah," Sarah confirmed. I held back my surprise as she added, "They're, like, together now or whatever."

"Won't they be tough to beat?" Josephine asked. Bonnie nodded beside her, seemingly wondering the same thing. "They're both really popular."

"Jake says we have the 'other' vote," I said. Then I started to get out of my seat. "I'm gonna go put my tray back. Sarah, walk me?"

She shot me a questioning look, but stood up anyway, and we walked across the cafeteria to dump our trays together.

"So Christine found your license in Sam's car and told me to tell you to back off, but something tells me most of that isn't very shocking to you," I sighed out. "What are you doing?"

"I thought we agreed not to talk about it," Sarah countered. "Wasn't that our agreement? You don't talk about your dates, and I don't talk about mine."

"Hooking up in his car doesn't really seem like a date. More like a booty call."

She shot me a venomous look, and I glared back, resisting the urge to back down. Arguing with Sarah made me nervous, and it always felt like she'd won even when she hadn't.

"I have it under control," she told me. "He's only dating Christine because he thinks he can't have me."

"Except he already *has* had you, hasn't he?" I bit out, and then turned and walked away before she could see how quickly I'd regretted that comment. I hated hurting her feelings, but it was hard to talk to her anymore at this point without bickering with her. Things felt so different between us now. Like there was so much tension between us that we had no choice but to snap at every opportunity.

Something was going to give soon, and I wasn't sure I was ready for the fallout.

Connor caught up to me in the hallway a few days later, after the final bell of the day rang, to tell me, "So Jake said today that I should tell you he's already gotten a surprisingly large amount of positive feedback with the Winter Formal thing. You and Sarah will probably get enough votes to be nominated in a few weeks, and then all you have to worry about is winning a head-to-head vote."

"Since when do you talk to Jake?" I asked, my eyebrows furrowing.

"Oh, uh... well, we don't. He just told me to tell you if... you know, if I saw you. He knows we're friends."

"But we aren't really friends," I deadpanned, still a little confused as Connor trailed after me.

"You know what I mean. He knows we talk."

"And apparently we aren't the only ones who talk," I said, shooting him a knowing look.

He rolled his eyes, casting a paranoid glance at the students around us. "C'mon, Katie. Stop."

"I didn't say anything," I insisted. "It's all in your head. I have no idea what *you're* thinking about, because everything in *my* head was totally innocent."

"Whatever," he dismissed, and sped up a little to catch me by the wrist and stop me in the hallway. I faced him, wary, as he asked, "Hey, what's up with you and Sarah? North Pole, much?"

"What does that even mean?" I shook my head and tried to keep walking, but he stopped me again.

"It means you guys are good at faking it at our lunch table, but I can tell she's still pissed at you, and she's not talking to me at all. Is she really still upset about that day you came over?"

I shrugged my shoulders. "Yeah, maybe. She'll get over it eventually."

"Well... you could tell her I just wanted to talk, you know. If she was mad because she thought I wanted to hook up, or whatever."

"Thanks, Connor. I will."

"No problem." He shoved his hands into his pockets and took a few steps backwards, away from me. "Work it out. I need stuff for my spank bank and if you guys break up I'll be running low on mental images."

"You're gross," I said flatly, meaning it, and he grinned and turned to jog away. "Posturing asshole," I mumbled.

I was still shuddering when I began my walk home five minutes later. I turned out of the school parking lot and got only a few feet down the sidewalk when I heard a voice calling after me, "Hey! Katie! Wait up!"

I paused and turned around to see Austin hurrying to catch up to me. I blinked, confused, but he just waved a hand as he came closer, then slowed to a stop right in front of me, panting.

"Hey," he breathed out. "Sorry, I just saw you walking and thought you might want a ride?"

I stared at him, taken aback. "Wait, you wanna give me a ride home?"

"If that's okay."

I searched his face for some sign that he was joking, but he seemed sincere. He pointed a thumb over his shoulder and told me, "I parked nearby, so it's not much of a walk to my car."

"Okay," I finally agreed. Austin was ultimately harmless, and he looked like he genuinely didn't mind spending some time alone with me.

We turned back together and began the walk to his car, and I could hear him still struggling to slow his heavy breathing. "I, like, sprinted after you," he told me with a small laugh. "It was kind of on instinct."

"So you *don't* have some massive, life-changing news for me? I'm disappointed," I admitted.

"Well, I could rub my new girlfriend in your face," he suggested, "but I thought that'd be rude. And ultimately pointless, considering you probably don't care what I do or who I date."

"I care," I said. "I'm glad you found someone else." Silently, I wondered if it was the girl from the party, but I didn't ask him aloud. I guess it didn't really matter much who it was.

"She's really cool. I think you'd like her. You should meet her, you know... eventually. She goes to a different school."

"How eventually?" I asked, casting a curious look his way. He was talking like he planned on having me in his life at some point in the future.

"I don't know. We'll see." He shrugged his shoulders, and we reached his car. I slid into the passenger's seat and inhaled. I'd been in this car almost as much as I'd been in Sarah's, but it felt different now. I could smell the faint remnants of a perfume that wasn't mine, but that was nice. I liked that it wasn't the same.

"Remember how to get to my house?" I joked.

"I think so," he said, playing along. "You know, I'm surprised Sarah doesn't give you rides every day. I used to."

"We've been going through a rough patch," I told him. I don't really know why I bothered, given that I hadn't had more than one or two real conversations with Austin in four months. But he'd always been a good listener. Easy to talk to. And it was funny... Austin had been a real boyfriend and Sarah was a fake girlfriend, but what I was going through right now with Sarah felt a lot like the beginning of the end of Austin and me had. So I guess it seemed like he'd understand better than anyone else would.

"I'm sorry to hear that," he said, and I sensed that he genuinely meant it. He was different from the Austin I'd talked to in the parking lot right after Sarah and I had begun our fake relationship. This Austin *acted* like he had a new girlfriend. He was happier. Lighter. "You're not breaking up, though, are you? You guys have been inseparable since, like, second grade."

"I don't know," I admitted. "I just don't want the fighting to end up getting worse and worse. Like how it was-"

"What, when we ended things?" he finished.

"Yeah," I said. Then I let out a sigh. "You know, I'm starting to wonder if all romantic relationships should just be avoided. Becoming a couple just complicates everything. Maybe I should've just stayed single forever; that way I'd never wind up disappointed or heartbroken."

"But that's no fun," he countered. "The good times are worth the bad ones, if you're really in love."

"What, so if you could do it all over again, you wouldn't change us dating? Even though it ended so terribly?"

"Of course not. I liked being with you. I mean, the whole dumping thing sucked, and it was really hard gathering the confidence to ask someone else out because I was terrified of more rejection... but, I mean, I've been with Nicole for just a few weeks and it was already worth the risk of having her turn me down."

I stared at the dashboard in front of me as he slowed his car to a stop at a red light. I tried to make sense of his logic. "So you're a 'you miss one-hundred percent of the shots you don't take' kind of guy," I said.

"Totally," he laughed out.

"But that's not an accurate metaphor," I insisted. "I mean, you miss a shot in a game, so what? That's not that bad. What if, like, I jumped out of a plane with a parachute on, and so then if it didn't open, I'd die? And the phrase was: 'Your parachute can't open if you don't pull the chord'? Like, I'd rather just stay on the ground and avoid jumping altogether. No chord or parachute necessary."

"But where's the fun in that?"

"I don't like heights," I told him. That made him laugh again.

"The rush is worth the fall, Katie! Nobody ever got anywhere because they sat at home being worried they'd get hurt. You need to fix things with Sarah. If she loves you and you love her, it'll work itself out. I think that's what we didn't have."

"And you have that with Nicole?" I asked.

He shrugged. "No idea yet. But I'd rather test the waters with her than never date again because of a fear of getting hurt." We reached another red light, and he faced me, a knowing look in his eyes. "You know, Oscar Wilde said it best: Hearts were made to be broken, Katie."

And I know he meant it to be inspiring, and that he was trying his best to help. But right then, sitting there alone with him and so very confused about my own feelings, I just thought that that was the lamest and most depressing thing I'd ever heard.

Chapter Eleven

The first one to find out the truth about Sarah and me – bar Owen, of course – was Jessa.

After all of the kissing and Sarah's speech in room 405 and the constant hand-holding, most of which was in some way initiated in an effort to keep Jessa in particular from finding out the truth, she was the first to find out anyway.

At the LAMBDA meeting that occurred the day before Winter Formal nominations, she spent almost the entire time glancing back and forth between Sarah and me. There was a look in her eyes that was a strange mixture of smugness and anger, and when the meeting ended, Sarah, still eager to keep her distance from me, immediately left.

Jessa, Jake, Violet, and I stayed late to work on Sarah and I's campaign, and when Jake and Violet left the room an hour later to go print out a second flier design, Jessa and I were left alone in room 405, her shuffling through a few photos Sarah and I had brought while I stood alongside her uncomfortably. It was strange, looking at the photos now. Most of them had been taken long before we'd ever pretended to be a couple, but a lot of those still looked like we'd already been together when they'd been taken.

Jessa finished looking the through the stack and let out an amused, "Very convincing."

I was lost in my own thoughts, not really paying attention to her, and mumbled an, "Mhmm."

She turned to me and arched an eyebrow. "Did you even hear what I just said?"

I blinked myself into the present and stared at her. "Sorry, what?"

She set the photos down and folded her arms across her chest. "I said that you guys are convincing. You and Sarah."

"What's that supposed to mean?" I asked.

She pursed her lips together, and her eyebrows rose higher. "Are you gay, Katie?"

"No," I retorted defensively, and then abruptly turned red. "I mean, yes. I just... I wasn't thinking, I meant-"

"I know what you meant," she interrupted with a shake of her head. "I think a part of me always knew. Just a gut feeling." I swallowed hard and stayed silent. I had an unpleasant inkling, deep in my chest, that we were caught no matter what I said.

It turns out I was right.

"I saw Sarah with Sam Heath out by the bleachers yesterday," she told me. "Either you're getting cheated on or I was right all along, so."

"I never wanted to hurt anyone," I said quickly, but she held up a hand to cut me off.

"I don't really care what you wanted. You're gonna hurt people regardless. And maybe this wasn't just some scam for you like it was for Sarah; I don't know. But what you both did is so insulting. And you deserve what's coming to you."

I bit down on the inside of my cheek. There was nothing I could really say to defend myself. She was right.

So I asked her, "Are you gonna tell Jake and the others?"

She glanced away from me, back to the photos, and lifted the stack of them again. Then she let out a slow breath, and tossed them back onto the table.

"Tell Jake and Violet I didn't feel well and went home. I can't be a part of this." I followed her with my eyes as she brushed past me and headed for the door. "But you two winning those crowns will be good for those of us who are *actually* gay. As much as I'd love to be proven right and to see you both humiliated, I'm not sure I want to give that up in exchange. But I do reserve the right to change my mind, especially if you don't actually win."

She paused, and then turned to look back at me. Then she shrugged her shoulders. "Plus... at least you're dedicated to playing the part well. Between kissing her, kissing *me*, and that really defensive 'no' you just gave me, you almost seem like an in-denial closet case. I guess karma's a bitch."

She smirked, and then disappeared from the doorway. As her footsteps faded, I stood alone in the center of the room, heart pounding hard in my chest. And then, instinctively, I reached for my phone.

My fingers shook as I found Sarah's number, and I felt tears in my eyes even though I didn't really know what was wrong with me. Jessa'd just told me she probably wasn't going to tell anyone as long as we worked hard to win the crowns, and yet here I was, freaking out anyway.

The phone rang once, twice, three times. And then, on the fourth ring, there was the click of Sarah answering, followed by heavy breathing. I heard a quick, "Shut up," and a low male voice say something in response, and then Sarah's was loud and clear as she asked, "Hello?"

I opened my mouth to speak, but the words didn't come. I couldn't stop hearing the heavy breathing. I felt like hyperventilating myself. It was like my brain was suddenly overloading with thoughts I'd been fighting for months to keep out, and I stood there in silence, the phone pressed to my ear so hard it hurt as I recognized Sam's low rumble of a voice. "Just hang it up, c'mon," he murmured.

There was a pause as Sarah moved her phone away from her ear and told him to shut up again. I guess she checked the caller ID, finally, because her tone immediately turned concerned and she asked, "Katie?"

"Oh, shit," Sam snickered quietly, and I heard a lot of abrupt shuffling. "Hang up!" he said, a bit louder.

"H-Hey," I forced myself to stutter out. Anything to distract myself from him. "Sorry. You're with Sam. I should go."

"No," she interrupted quickly. "Don't go. Are you okay?"

"I'm fine," I said. "Sorry. Again. Wrong number."

"You're full of shit," she replied.

I heard more shuffling, and then, "Oh, c'mon! Where're you going?" from Sam.

"I'm fine, Sarah," I repeated. "You can- I mean, you should stay with him, if that's what you want."

"Not if you need me," she insisted. She was being so nice, and I didn't know why. We'd mostly just been fighting lately, and she'd seemed to care so much more about Sam than about me.

"I just, uh..." I shook my head, hoping it would somehow rid me of the shaking in my voice. "Something happened and I'm a little- I'm okay, though."

"You don't sound okay. Where are you? Did someone say something to you?"

"It's fine." I was just trying hard not to let my imagination get the better or me. To convince myself that I'd only interrupted them kissing. It was taking a strange toll on my chest to think of what else they could've been doing. And it hurt even worse when it really, *genuinely* sank in that they'd obviously done it before in the past few weeks anyway.

"I swear to God, Katie, if you tell me you're fine one more time I'm gonna call your mom and get her to come help me look for you. Are you still at the school?"

"Fucking hell," I heard Sam sigh out in the background. "Just leave, then."

"Excuse me?" Sarah asked, moving the phone away from her mouth. I don't think either of them realized I could hear their conversation.

"I said you can leave," Sam retorted. He sounded annoyed. "Go take care of your *girlfriend*, then."

There was a long silence, and then Sarah's voice was loud next to her phone's mouthpiece again. "I'm gonna come pick you up. Give me fifteen minutes."

Violet and Jake didn't get back before Sarah, so I wrote them a note and left it on the table by the photos of us. Sarah watched me write it, her eyes moving back and forth between the paper beneath my fingertips and the stack of photos beside us, where Jessa'd left them on the table.

"I like this one," she finally said, lifting the one on the top of the stack with a small smile. "This was one of the ones you picked out?"

"If you don't recognize it," I mumbled. She'd provided most of the photos we were using, but I'd thrown in a few good ones. The one she was looking at was from sophomore year of high school. We were outside, posing for a picture by my mom's car just before a trip to the movies. Sarah's arm was wrapped around my waist, and I'd picked it because my eyes were on her and I had this indescribable expression on my face. Like I idolized her or something. I probably had back then.

"I love the way you're, like, staring at me in this picture," she murmured, setting the photo back down. "I wish a guy looked at me like that, you know?"

"Boys stare at you all the time," I told her, finishing the note and setting it aside. "You're just always too busy looking at Sam."

"Not always," she said, her gaze unmoving on me now. "What happened today?"

"Why do you care all of a sudden?" I asked her.

"I've always cared. You just stopped asking to hang out, and we stopped talking these past few weeks. That doesn't mean I wouldn't drop everything if you needed me."

I looked away from her. "Yeah, I guess. Gotta keep the girlfriend thing convincing."

"Uh, more like gotta make sure my best friend's okay," she corrected, her tone defensive.

"You didn't care that I was okay when you were throwing me into this stupid plan just so you could sleep with a guy you didn't know. Well, mission accomplished: Was it worth it?"

Her jaw tensed as she clenched her teeth together, and for a moment, I couldn't quite read her. She looked angry, but I didn't sense it radiating off of her like I had in the past few weeks. Then she relaxed a little, and nodded her head. "Yeah. It was."

Now it was my turn to look angry. "Well, good. I'm glad it was worth it for you. Because now Jessa knows we lied about dating each other, and the only reason we're not about to get outed to the entire school is because we might have a shot at those Winter Formal crowns. Are you happy now?"

Her face fell, and she stared at me, baffled. "Wait... what?"

"You heard me."

Her eyebrows furrowed in concern. "Jessa knows? How?"

"The same way anyone has learned anything about what's really going on between the two of us. She saw you with Sam. And now she's keeping it a secret because if we win those crowns and don't reveal we've been pretending, it'll be good for the other gay students at our school. The real gay ones." I swallowed hard. "And I think she's right. The least we can do now, after everything we've done, is to try to win them for LAMBDA. Maybe we can do that and then in a few years we'll be able to convince ourselves we're good people."

Sarah glanced to the doorway behind me, and then down at her feet. I watched her swallow. "Okay," she said at last, and when she looked up at me again, her expression was determined. That was relieving. She knew she'd screwed up again, and, like before, she now knew it was her job to help un-screw it up.

So this was it. It was full speed ahead in a race against Sam and Christine for the Winter Formal crowns. If we won, there was a good chance Jessa'd leave us alone. If we didn't, we were done.

"Yeah. Let's win this."

Chapter Twelve

"So what exactly are we gonna do?" I asked Sarah later that day. "If we get the crowns, Jessa won't out us, but how do we make sure we win? Do we just leave it to Jake?"

She laid prone at the end up my bed, her lower stomach exposed as she stretched out on her back. An open book was perched precariously between her hands just a foot above her face. I didn't recognize it; she'd evidently finished the one she'd borrowed from the LGBT resource center and was now reading something new.

"I don't know," she mumbled, and after a pause, added, "Just relax. Since I got us into this, let me worry about it."

"Those are two very contradictory sentences," I pointed out. "And in case you've forgotten, we were in this position before, and it only worked out because we *made* out. I don't really feel comfortable letting you worry about it alone given that if we don't get those crowns you probably have no clue how to make this only *mildly* catastrophic for us, as opposed to, you know, majorly socially suicidal." She lowered her book and shot me a look.

"It's simple," she said. "We just have to play to our strengths. We're hot and people like us, and the only thing that'll change people liking us is if Jessa outs us. Which you said she won't. So as long as no one else finds out we're frauds we'll be fine." Her phone buzzed in her purse, and I sat up on the other end of the bed, curious.

"That's not Jessa, is it?"

She didn't respond. Instead, she found her phone and pressed a few buttons, read the message, and then tossed the device back into her purse all in the span of a few seconds.

"You're not replying?" I asked.

"It wasn't her," she told me, shifting her gaze to me. Suddenly, she looked serious. "Katie?"

"Mhmm?" I leaned back, abruptly feeling a little self-conscious.

"You know that if we don't win, I'm taking the blame for all of this, right? Like, I want to. So don't worry."

"I'm gonna worry," I countered. "And I'm gonna take half the blame. I went along with it."

"Why? It was my idea. You're practically a victim." She glanced away, at last, and closed the book in her hands as she mumbled, "One of many." I watched her as she let out a sigh and continued, "So Sam really *is* an asshole, isn't he? Did you hear him on the phone earlier?"

"According to my mom, this is somewhat normal teenage girl drama," I said, trying to reassure her. "I mean, maybe not the whole 'faking gay for attention' thing, but liking assholes? Definitely a thing."

"You've never liked the wrong person," she insisted. "Austin was harmless. Meanwhile, here I am, falling all over people who either can't or won't feel the same way. I'm gonna be alone forever... especially after all of this shit comes out. I can't believe he's dating Christine and I'm stuck being 'the other woman'." She sighed. "Actually, scratch me being alone forever... I'm just gonna be the other woman forever because no one thinks I'm worth being in a relationship with."

"That's not true, Sarah." She arched an eyebrow at me disbelievingly, and I smiled. "There're always guys from other schools who haven't heard of you."

"Bitch," she laughed out, fumbling for a pillow and tossing it at me. I deflected it with both hands and it bounced into her lap. She rested her book on top of it even as I glanced to the cover.

"So is that why you read your cheesy happy ending romances?" I guessed. "As some sort of wish fulfillment?"

"Possibly," she agreed, grinning. "And in case you were curious, the second one ended horribly, so this is number three."

"Wait, that one's gay, too?" I leaned forward to get a better look. "Is that a vampire on the cover? *Really?*"

"I figured the ones that looked like they'd have happy endings haven't been ending well, so maybe if I picked something that looked dark, it'd surprise me."

"So you picked lesbian *Twilight*," I deadpanned. She laughed and hit me with a pillow again.

"God, you are so frustrating... but I'm glad you can make me laugh at a time like this."

"We really are screwed, aren't we?" I marveled. "We have so much work to do. I'm not quite as convinced we'll win as Jake seems to be."

"Just let me do the talking," she said. I scoffed.

"No way. Like I said: Last time I let you handle things alone, we only didn't get caught right then because you mauled me with your lips," I reminded her wryly.

She smiled at me. "Like *I* said: I thought it went well." She got a pillow to the face for that. "What!? That was a compliment!"

"Shut up," I countered, and willed my cheeks to lose their red tint before she got a good look at me again.

I wasn't sure what I expected at school the next morning, but it wasn't, well... *nothing*. It wasn't to walk in through the front doors at seven-thirty to the same amount of glances I was used to by now, and to reach my locker peacefully with Sarah at my side without anything more than a few usual smirks sent our way. Jessa, seemingly, was keeping her word after all. As long as we did our best to win Winter Formal Queens, our secret was safe.

Sarah and I went our separate ways to our first classes of the day, but before class started, we were forced to listen to the morning announcements. I sat in my desk silently, stomach churning, as Principal Crenshaw's voice echoed through loudspeakers around the building. "The senior class nominations for Winter Formal King and Queen are in. In two weeks, anyone who chooses to do so at the dance may head to the polls and vote for the couple they wish to see crowned. In no particular order, our nominees are..."

He paused for suspense, and I bit my lip. I was sure Sarah and I would be nominated, and we definitely needed the nomination at this point, but I still wasn't looking forward to it. I didn't want the attention. But what I wanted was pretty irrelevant now. Jessa outing Sarah and me would ruin our reputations faster than Principal Crenshaw could say, "Sarah Cooper and Katie Hammontree."

A few of the students in the room clapped politely for my sake, but most of them just slouched in their chairs, eyes half-open. I couldn't blame them. It was first period.

"Christine Goddard and Samuel Heath," Principal Crenshaw continued. "Jasmine Buford and Curtis Draper. And last but not least... Ryan Calloway and Fiona Edgerton."

So that was that. Four couples: three straight and one gay. Sarah and I were nominated. Now it was just a matter of winning.

I got called into the principal's office right around the end of my second class period, and spent the walk there with my heart hammering in my chest. I was so paranoid and distrusted Jessa so much that I was sure I knew what was going on. She'd changed her mind and decided a straight couple winning was better than a fake gay couple winning, and had gone to Principal Crenshaw with the truth. Now he was calling us in to force us to withdraw on the grounds that we'd faked being a couple. I wasn't even sure that was something he was allowed to do, actually, but if it was, it was certainly what was going to happen.

Sarah was already in his office when I got there, hands folded in her lap as Principal Crenshaw motioned for me to take a seat beside her. His secretary closed the door behind me as I moved to sit down.

Crenshaw was an intimidating man, thin and lanky and sporting greying hair that made him look older than sixty when I estimated he was mid-fifties at most. "Hello, Katie," he said, and leaned forward in his seat once I was settled. I glanced over at Sarah, but she didn't meet my eyes. "How are you today?"

"I'm okay," I mumbled, heart sinking deeper in my chest. We were *so* screwed.

"I was just chatting with Sarah about your nominations this morning. How are you guys feeling about being up for Winter Formal King and Queen?"

"Um..." I glanced to Sarah again. She'd raised her head, now, and I could tell from the expression on her face that she was just as caught off guard as I was by his question. "Okay, I guess? I don't really know."

"I take it this isn't something you're very interested in winning, then?" he asked. This question was open to both of us, and Sarah answered before I could.

"No, we'd like to win."

His lips pressed together, and his eyebrows turned down. He didn't like that answer.

He leaned even further forward, like he wanted to share a secret with us, and told us, "I'm aware that there was quite the campaign to get you two nominated."

Sarah and I exchanged looks, and, at last, she agreed, "Yeah."

"You are aware we have a tradition here at Flowery Branch High, I take it? The crowns are typically won by male/female couples."

"You mean 'always'," Sarah corrected.

He tilted his head slightly. "Hmm?"

"They're *always* won by male/female couples."

"Ah." He let out a short, disingenuous laugh. "Yes. Exactly." He cleared his throat. "Well... I just wanted to call you both in here to talk about your options regarding the nominations."

"Options?" I repeated before Sarah could.

"Options," he confirmed. "You see... there are a lot of students at this school who have some growing up to do. You two seem like very nice girls, but you must understand that your nomination doesn't exactly come from a place of acceptance."

"Not completely, sure," Sarah cut in. "But we've had some people tell us that they genuinely want us to win."

He chuckled at that. "Yes, well, I'm sure there are a lot of students who'd like for you two to win. Particularly quite a few of the male students. However, I personally feel that having two females win the titles of Winter Formal King and Queen would be a little..." He paused, searching for a word, and then finished, "misleading. Like a prank. Your picture would go in the school yearbook, and we have parents funding the purchase of these books who have the maturity to-"

"-to be homophobic," Sarah cut him off. I shrank back in my seat, uncomfortable. I'd realized what was going on here right around the time she had. Jessa hadn't come to him; he was coming to us all by himself.

He let out a deep sigh, rubbing at his temples. "That's not what I'm intending to get across here. I'm saying that kids can be immature, and parents will understand that this was all a cruel prank, you see? I'd like to avoid making a mockery of what's meant to be a fun activity for the senior class every year."

"And us winning would be a mockery because we're both girls," Sarah filled in for him. "So you're about to ask us to drop out."

"I'm only concerned for the two of you," he explained. "The students that vote for you as a joke would-"

"If you were concerned for us," she interrupted, "you'd have stopped students from putting stickers with the word 'dyke' written on them into my girlfriend's locker. You'd have started punishing boys for harassing and catcalling us in the hallways and you'd have made the discounts on our tickets equal to the discounts for heterosexual couples *without* pressure from LAMBDA. You'd have made an effort to look into the complaint I made to the office *two months ago* about the nonstop text messages I've been getting from anonymous numbers that belong to students at this school."

"Now, Ms. Cooper-"

"You're not concerned for us at all," Sarah ranted, unaffected by his attempt to cut in. I was watching her with amazement now. She was absolutely *destroying* him.

"You just think we're a joke yourself, and so you can't comprehend the fact that not everyone at this school is gonna think the same way as you. And neither is every parent. Some of them will actually be glad to see their kids aren't a bunch of homophobic jerks. Look, Principal Crenshaw, this may be hard for you to understand, but one person with some power – such as yourself – happening to be homophobic doesn't mean that everyone else is.

We're not dropping out on your behalf, so can you please stop wasting our time and start getting to work on ending bullying or lowering the calories in our school lunches? I'm missing my Physics class right now and I'm really, *really* bad at science."

"I think you just turned me straight." Jake's eyes were wide with adoration, and he shook his head as he pulled Sarah into his arms and hugged her tightly. I grinned next to her along with the rest of the LAMBDA kids at Jake's lunch table.

"She was amazing," I told them. "I don't think I've ever seen a teenage girl stun a grown man into silence until today."

"So he didn't even do anything?" Hattie asked, smirking beside Jake. "He's all talk?"

"What could he do?" Sarah asked as Jake finally released his grip on her. "I didn't cuss and I didn't do anything that violates school policy, unless he wanted to try and get me on disrespect, and besides, that'd involve telling other people the exact circumstances of our meeting with him. I don't think he wants to directly out himself as a homophobe."

"You guys are so winning those crowns," Jake told us. "I wanna have a rally out in front of the school this Friday, okay? You two can speak out about how much good your winning will do to make the school a more accepting place."

"Sounds perfect," Sarah agreed before I could protest. I wasn't good with crowds. "I'll write up a speech."

"Great! I'll work out the details and the setup, and you two just worry about letting everyone know why they should vote for you. You guys are gonna crush your competition."

"I sure hope so," Jessa cut in without warning, arriving at the table with a thin smile on her lips. I felt Sarah tense beside me.

"We'll win," I promised firmly, more to Jessa than to anyone else. After my scare with Principal Crenshaw this morning, I wanted a guarantee from her that if we won the crowns she'd leave us be.

I got it in the look we exchanged as she took a seat. My eyes said "Just don't rat us out and I swear we'll win this" and hers said "Deal".

"Let's flip this school upside down," Jake declared. "They have no idea what's about to hit them."

I was surprised when Sarah asked if I wanted to hang out after school that day. But I accepted anyway, and as we rode to her house in her car together, I could feel an awkward tension rising.

Things still felt a little off between us, but I knew she was the source of the discomfort.

"Can I ask you something?" she asked me just minutes into our ride.

"I guess." I reached out to turn her radio down. "What's up?"

"Are you and Austin getting back together?"

I gave a small start, then shook my head uncertainly. "What? No. Why would we?"

"Well, you hung out with him recently or something, right?"

"No," I repeated. "Where did you hear that?"

"Why does it matter if it's not true?"

"Because someone's lying to you."

"So... you *didn't* get into his car after school?"

I relaxed back in my seat and sighed, realizing what she was referring to. "Oh."

"Yeah," she deadpanned. "Forget about that?"

"He gave me a ride home from school," I explained. "It wasn't a big deal."

"Reconnecting with exes is always a big deal."

"Not when he has a new girlfriend and I'm... not interested." I swallowed nervously.

"Oh yeah? Then who was the guy you were straightening your hair for a couple weeks ago, if it wasn't Austin? Connor?"

I scoffed at her. "What's with the third degree? You can relax; you're the only one cheating here."

"C'mon," she sighed out. "I don't wanna fight. We were finally getting along. I just thought... I don't know. If there *was* a guy, maybe you'd wanna share. I've talked about Sam way too much and I wanted to give you a chance to talk."

"If we talk about anything," I told her, "I want it to be about the texts you told Crenshaw you've been getting."

I saw her grip tighten on the steering wheel. "It's not a big deal. You got them too, right?"

"Yeah, but not nonstop for two months," I argued. "Are people still harassing you?"

"It's not that bad," she dismissed. "Don't worry about it."

"I'm your best friend," I reminded her. "I'm only going to worry more if you don't show me them. If they're not that bad, then let me see."

Her hands flexed, and the knuckles whitened and then went red again. At last, she let out a quiet sigh.

"Alright. Fine."

And so, ten minutes later, I found myself sitting across from her on her bed, scrolling through dozens of text messages on her phone from unknown numbers while she chewed on her lip next to me.

It was, frankly, horrifying.

She got everything I'd had sent to me and more. Inappropriate pictures from guys, messages calling her a slut, telling her to make up her mind, asking for sex acts... There were insults and rude come-ons and even a couple of messages that seemed to be from girls. Those told her she was just looking for attention, but even despite their relative accuracy, they were just as stinging to read as the ones from guys.

I stopped around halfway through them and stared, appalled, as I read aloud, "I knew you were a slut but I didn't know you gave STDs to *girls*, too. RIP Katie." I looked up at her. "These are all disgusting."

"Amazing how I thought being gay would be this easy, huh?" she joked, rolling her eyes and quickly taking her phone back.

"Why haven't you deleted them?" I asked her. "And for that matter, why are getting so many? It wasn't this bad for *me*."

"Because who would be mean to you, Katie?" she countered. "You're this sweet, quiet, blonde girl who wouldn't hurt a fly. People can pick on you, or they can pick on me. The choice is obvious."

"They're just jealous," I insisted, but she laughed my comment off.

"Yeah, right. Of what? You don't get it: Look at me. Look at the kind of person I am."

I stared at her, not sure what exactly she was trying to get at. "I *am* looking at you."

"I came up with this whole plan in the first place. I used *everyone*. And I couldn't even hold Sam's attention long enough to be more than someone he just hooked up with every now and then. I can't even hold my own *parents'* attention. And even now, the right thing to do about this whole mess would be to just come clean, but I can't bring myself to do that because I'm so worried about what people will think. Like there was ever any doubt that tons of people already hate me anyway."

"Fuck them," I replied.

"That won't solve anything," she joked quietly. I forced a smile when she did, and reached for her hand. Her thumb stroked over my fingers and I let out a slow breath.

"I know those phone numbers feel like a lot of people, but they won't matter in another year," I reminded her. "They're all stupid. They don't know you like I do, and like all of our friends do."

She squeezed my hand, and then tilted her head to one side as her eyes met mine. The corners of her mouth quirked upward into a small smile. "That's what I love about you, Katie. Half the time I think I could kill someone and you'd still be convinced everyone else was wrong about me." She paused, and then added, "But you know, in psychology, they call that 'Unconditional Positive Regard', and I'm pretty sure it's only meant for therapeutic settings. Otherwise it's just unhealthy."

"Then I'll gladly be unhealthy," I declared, and felt my heart skip a beat when her smile widened and she leaned in toward me.

Her chin found my shoulder and her arms slid around me, and I hugged her back as she pulled me so close I could feel her heart beating against mine. I felt my own pulse speed up, and then got nervous that she could feel it, too, which only made my heart beat faster.

I wanted to pull away from her, but I also wanted to sit there, pressed close to her, until the upcoming days had passed and the Winter Formal was over. I was tired of stress and drama and lies, and this here, me and her, was simple. We were two best friends connected at the chest, and I could smell her familiar lavender shampoo and feel her hand tightening on my back as her fingers pulled the fabric of my shirt into a clump in her palm.

And then her arms tightened against me and I felt her breathe tickle my ear on an exhale, and I squeezed my eyes shut tightly and tried to ignore my pounding heart.

And in that moment, I finally accepted that I was *that* loser friend who'd end up heartbroken and alone, and that Sarah and I were not simple at all. Maybe we'd never been. Maybe I'd loved her back when that photo of me staring at her had been taken back in sophomore year. Maybe I'd loved her back when we'd gone to Six Flags together as kids. Or maybe I hadn't.

But I certainly loved her now.

Chapter Thirteen

My bathroom mirror had a small, translucent spot on it near the bottom-left corner, and I stared at it with furrowed eyebrows for a moment, before leaning forward to rub at it until it was gone.

I leaned back and stood up straight, meeting my own gaze in the mirror. My hair was tied back in a messy bun, and I stared at the dark circles under my eyes as I reached up to tuck a strand of stray hair behind my ear. I took a deep breath and then let it out.

And then I mumbled, my voice barely a whisper, "I'm gay."

It didn't sound very convincing. I was much too nervous, and lacked any sign of confidence.

I cleared my throat and tried again, my voice louder and stronger this time. "I'm gay, and I'm in love with my best friend."

I bit my lip as the words hung in the air, and then let out a deep sigh and moved to turn the bathroom light off. "I'm so screwed."

I stared at the ceiling after I'd laid down on my bed, and the clock on my nightstand ticked closer to midnight. The revelation that I was officially In Love didn't make me feel the way I'd always imagined it would. Being in love was running slow motion through a field of flowers, or floating on a cloud, or hearing swelling romantic music every time Sarah kissed me. It wasn't supposed to involve an unpleasant sinking feeling in my chest. I felt lost and confused and totally alone, and I had a limited amount of people to turn to for help.

Sarah was out of the question for obvious reasons. Jake still didn't know the truth about Sarah and me, and neither did any of my other friends. My parents were a possibility, but I wouldn't be able to explain my exact circumstances to them, either. Owen was probably my best choice, but I'd need a ride to get to him, and my options there all had their pitfalls. I needed someone who was easy-access. Someone from school, and someone who knew the truth.

Oh, God.

Jessa was unamused when I walked into Room 405 and closed the door behind myself the next afternoon. I'd found her in the hallway earlier today and asked her to meet me here, and given the look she'd shot me in response, it was now a pleasant surprise that she'd actually shown up. As pleasant a surprise as Jessa's presence could be, anyway.

"Is this about you being paranoid I'm gonna start telling people the truth?" she asked me. "Because you can relax, provided the rally on Friday goes well."

"That's not it," I said. "I, uh... look, I think I'm in love with Sarah," I blurted out. She blinked at me. "I know I'm in love with Sarah," I corrected abruptly, feeling embarrassed. "I didn't know who else to ask for advice."

"Is this a trick?" she questioned, eyebrows furrowed. "Because if you really think-"

"Not a trick," I told her. "You, uh... when you said I sounded defensive the other day? You were right. I just... couldn't face it, I guess. Deep down I knew being gay probably meant loving her, and I didn't want to love her, but now and I do and she's straight and I've got this awful sinking feeling in my chest that won't go away no matter what I do and I don't know what I'm supposed to-"

"Whoa, Katie," she cut me off, looking appalled. "Shut up."

I fell silent and swallowed hard. Jessa let out a sigh.

"Look. I don't really care about you and Sarah's drama. I don't even like you guys," she said. My eyes found my feet, and there was a long silence. Jessa sighed again, sounding vaguely annoyed. "God, okay, you're pathetic. Just... tell me what you want from me."

"I couldn't talk to anyone else," I mumbled, avoiding her eyes. "You're the only one who knows the full story, and you know what it's like to like girls. I thought maybe you knew how I could get over her."

She raised an eyebrow at me. "So let me get this straight: You faked being a couple, you faked being attracted to each other, and you faked being gay. Now you're telling me you're actually gay and actually attracted to her, but she's straight and into Sam Heath and you're left sad and alone and you want a rebound?" She folded her arms across her chest. "I'm not gonna be your experiment, if that's what you're asking. I only said what I said and kissed you at that party to piss Sarah off."

I felt my cheeks heat up. "That's not-"

"Although, come to think of it," she interrupted, looking a little amused, "it worked, didn't it? She was all over you. I am kind of curious about what happened after she dragged you away." My cheeks went redder, and she seemed a little surprised. "*Really?*"

"We were a little tipsy," I murmured.

"I never thought I'd say this..." Jessa admitted, and paused to shake her head before finishing, "...but what makes you so sure she's totally straight?"

I opened my mouth to answer, and then paused abruptly, stumped. "I mean... she's just always... she-" I paused again. "Huh."

"Pretend for a second that I actually give a shit about you and Sarah and that we're being optimistic. What else has happened?"

I blinked a few times, wracking my brain. "Um, she canceled her first date with Sam to come pick me up when she thought I was on a date with a guy. She was pretty pissed afterward." Jessa motioned for me to keep going. "I don't know. Um. She likes lesbian fiction? I don't know if that's a sign; I'm sure plenty of straight girls are into it too." I paused again. "Oh, she left Sam to come pick me up. Again. She chooses me over Sam more than I realized, actually."

I furrowed my eyebrows, hardly daring to believe there was a possibility that I wasn't just harboring a one-sided crush. Of course she cared about me. We'd been best friends for a decade. And sure, she'd had a crush on Sam for a while, but she was still a good person, and a good person would choose a lifelong friend over a boy she was casually hooking up with. And she'd been so keen on getting my opinion on what she was doing with Sam because friends were like that. They sought advice from each other.

"Just throwing this out there," Jessa spoke up, looking amused, "but how hilarious would it be if she's been spending this whole time screwing him because she assumed you weren't into her? Like... you fake this thing, right? And then you kiss and you both enjoy it, things are tense, she gets some kind of vibe that you're probably not interested, and throws herself at Sam to help put this new thing with you out of her mind?" She let out a breath, marveling at herself. "Shit, I hate you guys. This'd never happen to me."

"Or me," I corrected her. "That's not how it went, okay? I'm the freak who caught feelings. She's been all about Sam since freshman year. She puts me over him because she's a good friend."

"Yet your 'good friend' asked you to spend your senior year faking lesbianism with her."

"That doesn't make her a bad friend. She just makes bad decision sometimes," I argued. "She's going to make up for it. She wants to."

"Whatever. Look, you asked for my opinion. I don't like you or Sarah-"

"Yeah, I got that."

"-but I don't think it'd be a longshot to tell her how you feel. Is she still hooking up with Sam now that he's running for the Winter Formal thing with Christine?"

I shook my head. "I don't think so."

"So then your chances just went up. I mean, I'm all in favor of you two becoming a real couple. For one, it's better for LAMBDA, and secondly, it removes two awful people from the dating pool by sticking them with each other. Win-win."

"Thanks, Jessa," I sighed out.

She shrugged her shoulders and moved to leave the room. "Look, you wanted my opinion. You have it now, so leave me alone. Bye."

The door slammed shut behind her, and I rested my face in my hands, groaning loudly.

I couldn't spend time with Sarah in the days that followed without feeling uncomfortable. Despite getting along with her better than I had in the past few weeks, realizing my feelings for her had made things awkward for me, to say the least. I felt guilty constantly.

When she held my hand and gave it an innocent squeeze, I felt remorse for the tingles in my hand and the butterflies in my stomach. When she hugged me, I took care to not squeeze too tight for fear she'd somehow realize how I really felt. And forget kissing. That went out the window the day after our talk in her bedroom. Sarah got the point after the first time I turned my head in the hallway so that her lips would meet my cheek, and she'd been a little off ever since, which only made me more paranoid that she'd realized why I was avoiding being affectionate with her.

I started sweating bullets the morning of the rally when Sarah asked me, "Hey, so what's been up with you lately?" We were in her car on our way to school. Jake and the others were already waiting for us; the rally was to be staged in front of the school in the minutes leading up to the morning bell.

"What do you mean?" I asked, feigning ignorance. I didn't dare look at her; my eyes stayed glued to the passenger's side window.

"I don't know. I guess... you've been kinda distant since the other day in my bedroom. Did I do something wrong?"

I struggled for words even as we pulled into the school parking lot. "...No. No, you didn't. I guess I'm just having a weird week. All of this Winter Formal drama..."

Sarah parked her car and shifted toward me. When she spoke, her words were rushed and she looked nervous. "If you don't want to kiss anymore, we don't have to, but I think we might need to for the rally. I don't want to make you uncomfortable."

My stomach lurched, and I think it showed on my face, because Sarah bit her lip and sighed.

"God, that's it, isn't it? You're over this."

"It's exhausting," I admitted, "but I don't think I'm allowed to be over it. I just... wish it didn't feel so heavy. It feels like the fate of every gay teen in the world is on our shoulders just because of some stupid Winter Formal thing. I didn't expect to feel so much pressure."

"This is how we give back," she said, reaching out to touch my shoulder. I flinched and she moved away. "C'mon, Katie. Talk to me. What's bugging you? So you wish we didn't have to do this anymore, okay. But that doesn't explain why you practically jump every time I touch you."

I shook my head. The words were on the tip of my tongue, but I knew I wouldn't be able to get them out. It'd ruin us if she didn't feel the same way.

"Let's just get the rally done," I said instead, dodging her question. "You give your speech, we kiss, they cheer, and everyone's happy. Problem solved."

"Not for me," she protested, but I'd already moved to get out of her car. I fast-walked to where Jake stood at the front of the school, fliers in his hands and a podium at his side.

"You guys really went all-out," I observed. There was even a microphone on the podium.

"I've got a friend that does tech for the Drama Club," Jake informed me. "He hooked us up. Is Sarah's speech ready?"

"You'll have to ask her," I mumbled, glancing Sarah's way. She was stalking toward us and she didn't look happy.

"One second, Jake," was all she said, and then she was pulling me aside and lowering her voice even as I pointedly looked away from her. "Look, I get the hint, okay? I get it. Look at me."

I blinked twice, not understanding her, and then forced my gaze to hers at last. To my surprise, she looked near tears.

"I'll do the speech. We have to give the crowd a show. Maybe we'll do it again if we win the crowns. And then it's over. We do the breakup plan and then we move past this. We can forget it ever happened. Okay?"

I stared at her. My heart was pounding in my chest now. She 'got it'. She knew. She knew how I felt and she wanted out now. She wanted to forget this ever happened.

I swallowed hard and nodded, my heart plummeting into my stomach. To know that Sarah still wanted to be friends after all of this was only mildly relieving when I also knew that she didn't have the same feelings for me that I had for her. I felt sick, and for a moment, I was glad I'd left the whole speech to Sarah.

Jake, Violet, Hattie, and the other LAMBDA members with fliers had managed to attract a crowd of students in front of the school, and now Jake came to Sarah, microphone in his hand.

"I think we've got a big enough group. More people will show up to see what's going on, but I think now's a good time to start. Are you ready?"

Sarah swallowed a lump in her throat. She looked as sick as I felt, which was strange, as I'd never known her to have stage fright. She was probably reacting to the realization that I loved her.

That thought had me nearly making a run for it, but Jake wrapped an arm around me right then and guided me to Sarah. I stood next to her, forcing a smile as she retrieved a stack of note cards from her pocket. "Good morning, guys," she greeted. Like me, she put on a happy face for the crowd. "Any of you that've gotten fliers can probably guess what this is about. Katie and I are in the running for the Winter Formal crowns this year, and we need your votes to make a difference."

She was reading off of her note cards now, and I watched her scan her own writing before glancing to the crowd again. "Having a lesbian couple win these crowns will show not only how far we've come as a society, but will also show the world that gay couples are just like any other couple. We love the same way, we have the same feelings-"

"Only you're hotter!" a guy at the front of the crowd shouted. A few people laughed and clapped, and I rolled my eyes. It felt inevitable at this point that we'd get interruptions like that.

But Sarah reacted differently. She glanced up, located the boy who'd shouted, and stared at him for a long while, almost to the point of discomfort. I noticed her jaw had tensed. At last, she looked away, took a deep breath, and put her note cards back in her pocket.

"Actually, you know what?" she began again, diplomatic tone gone. "*This* is why we need a lesbian couple to win this thing. Because of stuff like this. But it doesn't mean anything for us to just win it. Any idiot can just vote for two girls he has no respect for just because he thinks they're hot. We need people to vote for us because they recognize that we're no different from anyone else. *I'm* no different from anyone else, Katie's no different from anyone else, and neither are any of the other gay kids that go to our school. And they deserve the same respect that all human beings do. They deserve the same respect that they were given before they came out. I'm the *same person* I was before I told everyone I was bisexual!"

She paused, then, and this time the crowd was silent. I watched her take a deep breath, and then shake her head. "No, that's a lie. I'm a better person. Before I fell for Katie, I thought the same

231

way I'm sure plenty of you all do. I thought gay guys were shopping buddies and I thought gay girls had it easy. But I happen to know that my friend Jake hates shopping, and these past few months have been the hardest of my life. Being gay isn't easy. Being bi isn't easy. I wasn't exactly loved by everyone before I came out, but I didn't know that I could be hated by as many people as I've felt hated by since. And I didn't do anything! I just loved another girl." She looked to me, and I stared back. I couldn't look away. There was something in her eyes I'd never seen before. "I just love another girl," she corrected quietly. "I'm so sick of being punished for it."

The crowd faded into the background as I looked back at her. No one else existed; the dozens of pairs of eyes staring at us were gone. This speech, I knew, was the most honest she'd been since we'd started this whole charade, and I could see an openness in her face that I hadn't seen in a long time. I was caught up in the moment and even more caught up in her. She was looking at me like... like...

I kissed her.

Really kissed her. Not a nervous first kiss in front of thirteen strangers. Not a peck in the hallway. Not even a passionate make out session like the one we'd had in the bedroom at Justin Barnes's party. It was like time had stopped. My hands were on her cheeks, drawing her closer, and hers fumbled for my waist. She hadn't been expecting it; I'd caught her off-guard. But she was kissing me back anyway. Was it for the crowd, or...?

We parted before I was ready and she moved in to kiss me again, catching my bottom lip between both of hers. I forced myself to stop thinking. Sarah was kissing me and I could feel her whole body pressed into mine and she was *still* kissing me and she was so soft and *still* kissing me and I never wanted to stop.

But we did. We parted to catcalls and wolf-whistles and my heart promptly sank back to my stomach again. Jake moved in awkwardly and took the microphone from Sarah, offering the crowd a meek wave. "Alright, thanks for coming, guys! Vote for Katie and Sarah!" And then, when the crowd had begun to disperse, he shot the two of us an amused look; a silent *"Really?"*

"I have to go," Sarah mumbled, and hurried away from me without another word.

"Shit," I hissed. I tried to follow her, but the crowd caved in around me and made it impossible. Jake caught my arm and moved to walk into the school with me.

"What was that?" he asked. I colored.

"The kiss? We were just- I just thought-"

"Not the kiss; I *get* the kiss. What I don't get is why Sarah looked so spooked afterward."

"It's complicated," I told him, because "*she just realized that I love her and now I kissed her like the world was about to end and she feels too guilty to turn me down*" seemed like an inappropriate explanation.

Jake shook his head. "Girls. Thank God I'm gay. I'll see you later?"

"Definitely," I confirmed with a nod of my head. As soon as he was gone, I let the panic I felt fully set in. As hard as it would be, there was only one thing I could do now: apologize until I was blue in the face.

Sarah avoided me for the duration of the day. She even skipped lunch so that she wouldn't have to see me. As the hours wore on, I was more and more confident that I'd ruined our friendship.

"I should've let her initiate the kiss," I murmured to myself as I walked out to the school parking lot at three o'clock that day. "I'm such an idiot."

"Hey! Katie!"

I paused, wincing to myself as a voice called out to me. Who would it be this time? Jake, here to insist on more Winter Formal advertising? Austin, with more love life advice? Sarah, ready to dump me and end our friendship once and for all?

Jessa jogged up to me, only slightly out of breath, and looked somewhat exasperated as she handed me a piece of paper. "Jake wanted me to give this to you. Show it to Sarah, too. It's another idea for a flier."

"I really don't care," I deadpanned. "Print whatever you want. Paste it on every locker. I'm just sick of seeing those pictures of Sarah and I."

"Damn, with all that bitterness you had to have gotten dumped," she guessed. "That sucks. Could've sworn she was into you."

"Yeah, well, she's been avoiding me all day, so I guess you have to settle for me being miserable. I just want to win those crowns and get it over with."

"How'd you screw up?" she asked, looking genuinely curious.

"What do you care? You don't even like me, remember?"

"Yeah, but I enjoy lesbian drama every now and then."

"She's not a lesbian."

"Well, obviously."

I rolled my eyes, eager to get away from her. "Look, we had a moment in her bedroom the day before I came to you about all of this. I was afraid she'd figure out I liked her so I tried to back off a little, but we had another moment at the rally when I kissed her and she freaked. So now she knows I like her and doesn't want anything to do with me."

"That doesn't sound like the reaction of a good friend to me," Jessa pointed out, amused.

"Yeah, well... maybe you were right, then. Maybe she's not a good friend."

"I don't believe you really think that for a second." She folded her arms across her chest and smirked. "God, you're dumb. This is painful to watch, honestly."

"Then go. I don't have time for this." I shoved the flier into her hands and turned away.

"You should go talk to her."

"Tried that," I called back as I walked away. "Like I said: She's avoiding me."

"So go to her house. I'll give you a ride."

I paused and turned to face her, raising an eyebrow. Her arms were crossed again, and she wouldn't quite look at me. My other eyebrow went up. "Wow. Jessa Underwood has a heart?"

"Shut up. You know I get something out of this."

"We can win the crown either way, fight or no fight," I pointed out. "You want us to make up."

"I want you to *shut up*," she repeated. "Look. As much bad as you guys have done... you're doing some good, too. You two *actually* falling in love with each other would fall under that category. This is totally selfish on my part. It benefits the rest of us."

"You know... maybe you and Sarah would get along better than you think," I remarked.

She looked unconvinced. "Yeah? Why is that?"

I tilted my head to the side and smirked back at her. "You're both overly fond of happy endings."

As soon as I was out of her car, Jessa put the gear into reverse and began to back out of Sarah's driveway. "Wait," I called after her, panicking. "How am I supposed to get home?"

"I guess we'll find out," she replied, winking at me. I grit my teeth, mentally cursing her as she drove away.

Given that my house was several miles away and I was lacking a vehicle, I couldn't back out now. Sarah's house loomed overhead, suddenly looking about twice its usual height. Intimidated, I took several moments before I finally forced myself to go knock on the front door. Sarah's parents, as usual, weren't home, and so it was up to her to answer. Therefore I wasn't very surprised when no one came to the door.

Sighing, I settled down on the ground, my back against the door, and rummaged through my purse until I found my cell phone. My mom would be home from work soon, and I wasn't too far away. She'd be willing to come pick me up.

I sighed, abandoning that plan abruptly. She'd know Sarah hadn't been willing to give me a ride home, and then I'd never hear the end of questions from her. Jake provided the same dilemma. But maybe Austin was an option.

I only hesitated for a moment before I dialed his number. He picked up on the third ring.

"Hello?"

"Hey, Austin. It's Katie."

There was a short pause before he replied. "Katie? Hey..."

"Look, I just... I'm kind of stuck somewhere and..." I shook my head, realizing how stupid I sounded. I'd dumped him. Now I wanted his help because it was convenient. "I'm sorry," I amended. "Never mind. Don't worry about it."

"It's cool, Katie. What's going on? Do you need a ride?"

"I can probably just ask my mom," I insisted, although I knew I wouldn't.

"It's seriously fine. I just got home; I'm not doing anything."

As he spoke, I sighed aloud again. Mid-sigh, the front door swung open and I fell backwards, my sigh morphing into a gasp of surprise. Lying on my back, I saw Sarah standing over me, her eyebrows furrowed.

"Um... I've gotta go. I swear I'll be fine; I'll text you if I end up needing your help, okay?"

"You sure?"

"Yeah. Bye." I hung up and hurried to my feet as Sarah closed her front door behind me. Her cheeks were tear-stained and her eyes were red-rimmed. She'd been crying, and I didn't understand why.

"Why would you come here?" she asked me.

I bit down on my lip. My heart was already starting to pound. She was starting in on me like *I* was the one she expected to be antagonistic. "I just wanted to talk," I murmured, feeling very, very small.

"So talk."

I glanced to her eyes again to see that her gaze had hardened. Maybe this hadn't been such a good idea after all. "I uh... I get why you'd want to push me away, okay? But... I still want to be your friend. That's all we have to be, right? It's like you said... we can just get through the dance and then start the breakup stuff." I waited with baited breath for her answer. Her gaze stayed on the floor and she sighed.

"Then why would you kiss me the way you did at the rally today?"

I swallowed hard. "I was just caught up in the moment. I didn't mean for you to get upset-"

"Well, I did," she cut in harshly. "I feel like you used me because you want to win the crowns so that Jessa won't tell everyone the truth."

I shook my head. Now she was officially not making any sense. "What?"

"Putting on a big show in front of the crowd like that," she clarified, sniffling quietly. "I was trying hard to be honest today. I meant everything I said, and I meant that kiss. But I saw the way you were looking at me, Katie. You were totally spooked."

"*You* were spooked," I corrected, and then shook my head again. "Wait, *what*?" Meant what she said? Meant the kiss?

"You love me?" I asked, dumbfounded. "But I love you."

"No, *I* love- what?"

We stared at each other, Sarah, for all her intelligence, about two steps behind me. I felt a grin pull at the corners of my lips. *God*, was I dumb. "Sarah, I love you. I'm sorry it took me so long to figure out. I spent a lot of time panicking and denying it because I was worried about getting rejected. I thought you were into Sam."

"I was." She shook her head, wide-eyed, and corrected, "I mean, I thought I was... until I kissed you. Sam was just another cute guy after that. I only hooked up with him because I thought you didn't like me."

"But I told you I didn't think you should be with him," I pointed out, my mind reeling. This felt like a dream. Maybe it was. I pinched myself to check, and let out a sigh of relief when it hurt. We were actually having this conversation.

Sarah, more than anything, just looked amused now. "No, that's not what happened, Katie. *I* tried to bring up the kiss. *I* tried to bring up the party. I even asked you if you really thought it was a good thing that I was talking to Sam!"

"And I told you it wasn't!"

"No, you said 'great'! I remember; it was the morning after the party. You were happy I was talking to him and you gave me your approval. So after that I was sure there was no way you were confused like I was. So I went after Sam. Then when you went back on that, I called you out and you still just insisted Sam was a bad guy. I gave you so many chances."

"Well..." I hesitated, thinking back. And then I deflated. She was kind of right. "...Sorry?"

"Apology accepted. God." She stepped toward me, closing the distance between us and kissing me. I blinked, wide-eyed, and then pulled her impossibly close to kiss her back. This was happening. This was *happening.*

She rested her forehead against mine when she parted, and, grinning back at me, explained, "So when we did this earlier today, after you'd been avoiding me... I thought you knew. I thought you knew how I felt after the night in my bedroom, and I thought that that was why you hadn't been kissing me lately. When I told you we could end it all this morning, I thought I was doing you a favor."

"I thought it was your nice way of rejecting me," I admitted. Then I chuckled as a thought struck me.

"My parents are going to freak. They're convinced I'm in love with you."

She pulled away suddenly, looking serious. Her hand squeezed mine. "They knew you were gay because you are," she realized.

"I think that kind of comes with being in love with your best friend," I acknowledged. "Yeah."

"I'm not," she admitted. "Gay, I mean."

"Yeah, I know." I smiled at her. "I don't care what you are. Bi, straight with an exception... whatever."

She chewed her lip for a moment, and I raised an eyebrow, realizing she was going to elaborate. "I spent some time alone with Hattie. We talked a lot." She saw the look I was giving her and emphasized, "Talked. That's all. Anyway, she's bi and I was playing the role, saying what I thought I should as someone who was pretending to be bisexual too... and it fit. It just felt right. I think I could love anyone. I mean... if I can go ten years with you without being aware of my own feelings, the possibilities are kind of endless."

"I knew," I admitted. "Deep down. I'm looking at you like you're the only thing that matters in half of those pictures we're using for the fliers. I never liked Austin. I just did whatever you did to feel normal. It took an awkward conversation or two to face the truth."

"I wish you'd told me."

"I wish *you'd* told me," I countered.

242

She smiled shyly. "Yeah, well... those damn books screwed me up."

"Oh, did they?" I laughed out. "Sad endings scarred you? I guess you should've picked up the erotica after all."

"It wasn't even that, okay? Book number 1: one of the girls realizes she's straight. Book number 2: one of the girls realizes she's bi and loves a guy, and the other girl ends up alone. Book number 3: they both get murdered by vampires."

"That sounds so dark for lesbian *Twilight*."

She punched my shoulder, giggling. "No matter what I picked up, there was always someone who got screwed over. I didn't want to end up like that. I mean, have you seen how it ends for Dana and Alice?"

"Dana and Alice date? What?"

"Oh, you hadn't gotten that far? I'm sorry. Spoilers."

"Oh my God," I laughed out, shaking my head. "We are so strange. Please kiss me."

"Well, if you insist."

Chapter Fourteen

With Winter Formal just around the corner, things were a little... complicated. Sarah and I had been a fake couple that everyone thought was a real couple, and now we were a real couple that everyone thought was a real couple but that *Jessa* knew had been a fake couple at one point. Our friends at lunch noticed the difference, too. We didn't force touches and pecks anymore; we just did them because we could. And I didn't want to stop doing them. I could kiss Sarah whenever I wanted, without any excuses. And she'd always kind of been into PDA.

"I've gotta say, guys... I'm glad you two feel this comfortable around us now after three months of dating, but I'm trying to eat."

I pulled away from Sarah shyly and shot Hannah an apologetic look, but luckily she was smirking at us with amusement.

"I wondered when Sarah would sway Katie on the whole PDA thing," Dina remarked, looking to Josephine. "Clock it at what, about eleven weeks?"

"Sorry," I hurried to say, before they could get in any more digs. Sarah shot me a wide smile and I had to hide one of my own.

"Aw, look at them. They're proud of their grossness," Josephine declared. "That's adorable."

"Shut up," Sarah shot back, but her hand squeezed mine under the table, and I couldn't hide my smile this time.

My parents found out about us three days later, when they got home earlier than expected after a night out together and caught Sarah and I on my bed with my shirt half up over my head. So that was fun.

They sat us down on the couch and gave us this long lecture about safe sex – though I was pretty sure they knew just as little about lesbian sex as I did – and then sent Sarah on her way, much to my chagrin. Then Dad high-fived me when Mom's back was turned. Neither of them seemed very surprised, and I decided that maybe they didn't need to know about the whole fake-gay-relationship-turned-real-gay-relationship thing. My home life was a lot less complicated that way.

They were gone the next night, as well, and I was more nervous than I'd ever been for Sarah to come over. We hadn't gotten farther than the singular attempt to get my shirt off, and tonight seemed like a likely time. I wanted my first time with a girl to be special.

I waited for her in the living room, clicking through television channels to pass the time, and she entered without ringing the doorbell, a stack of board games under one arm. I raised an eyebrow at her. "You brought board games?"

"Just in case you didn't want to do other stuff," she elaborated. "I know it's all new to you. I mean... it's new to me too, of course. I don't know. Last night was..."

"Nerve-wracking?" I filled in.

"Yeah," she laughed out nervously. "I mean, it was good, I just don't... actually know anything. About anything. Which I'm not used to."

"Welcome to my world," I acknowledged, sweeping an arm as though introducing the living room to her. "I might as well be a sexless amoeba."

"You're cuter than an amoeba." She collapsed beside me on the couch, smiling over at me. "Wanna just watch a movie?"

"Maybe."

"Okay. It's your turn to be big spoon, though."

"I hate being big spoon."

"Well, you'll just have to deal." She stretched out her legs and cuddled into me, and I settled on a channel five minutes into some eighties horror movie. I didn't really pay attention to it. Being with Sarah like this was unlike anything I'd never felt before. Yes, there'd been Austin, but hanging out with Austin felt like hanging out with a friend who had a crush on me. When I was with him, it was a chore, and when we did anything past kissing I'd just wanted it to be over as quickly as possible. But I wanted to sit here with Sarah forever.

I laid my head on hers for a moment and told her, "You smell nice."

"You feel nice," she whispered back.

"You look nice," I countered quickly.

"You taste nice," she shot back, almost accusingly. When I gave her a questioning look, she stuck her tongue out to touch my neck.

"Gross!" I wiped it off with my hand and flicked her in the bicep.

"You started it," she mumbled, burying her face into my neck again. I relaxed into her and closed my eyes. "Neither of us are watching this movie," she admitted a few minutes later.

"Nope," I agreed.

She raised her head and kissed my cheek, then tilted my chin with her hand until we were face to face, our noses nearly touching. "Would it totally freak you out if I wanted to go up to your bedroom?"

"I don't know," I said instinctively.

"Your heart rate says yes," she joked, gesturing to where her chest was pressed to mine. "Or maybe that's mine; I can't tell."

"Why are you nervous?" I asked, brushing her nose with mine. "It's me."

"That's why I'm nervous. Things are so nice with you. They're perfect. I want this to be, too. What if I screw it up? I mean, I've screwed everything *else* up."

"No, you haven't."

She shifted, sitting up and facing me. "Yeah, I kind of did. I shouldn't have spent so much time on Sam. Or *any* time on him. I knew he was an ass, and I knew you were right. I didn't know how you felt, but I knew he was using me and I knew it was wrong to hook up with him. If I'd just listened to you we wouldn't have fought as much as we did."

"If I'd told you I liked you we wouldn't have, either," I pointed out.

"Yeah, but you can't be blamed for that. You didn't know how I felt."

"And *you* didn't know how *I* felt. So we're even as far as I'm concerned."

She chewed at her lip for a long moment, then leaned forward to kiss me. My eyes fluttered shut, and then opened when she pulled away. But instead of moving away from me, she came forward again and kissed my cheek, then my jawline, and then my neck. I let out a shaky breath and rolled my head to one side. I couldn't think, and breathing was getting harder.

She kissed back up to my lips and then watched me, smiling faintly as I looked at her with half-lidded eyes. "Dazed?" she whispered, amused.

"And confused," I confirmed.

"Hey." She leaned in to kiss me again, and then pulled away and moved her lips to my ear. "Thank you for being so perfect. I don't think I deserve you."

I wound my arms around her and pulled her closer. "You deserve me. Thank you for the fake relationship idea."

She giggled into my ear. "Bet you thought you'd never say that, huh?"

"Let's go to my room," was my response.

"Hate to say I told you so..." Jessa teased, catching up to me at my locker the day before the Winter Formal. I'd seen her at LAMBDA meetings before now, but this was the first time she'd caught me alone since Sarah and I had begun dating.

"Well, I am happy to say you told me so," I joked, smiling over at her. "Thank you for being supportive... in your own, you know, not at all supportive way."

"So you're gay," she stated. "And Sarah's...?"

"Bisexual."

"Okay." She looked thoughtful for a moment. "I think I could like you guys."

"We're not open for threesomes," I remarked.

"Ha ha. Hilarious. I meant I might like you *as people*. With enough time. God knows it'll make LAMBDA meetings less hellish. Everyone else there worships you two so I might as well jump on the bandwagon."

"You only like us because we actually turned out to be gay?" I asked her, feigning a gasp. "Doesn't that make you a little... *heterophobic*?"

"Oh, shut up," she replied, rolling her eyes at me. I grinned back at her. "Just win the crowns tomorrow night, you big faker."

"That's the plan," I confirmed. Jessa waved goodbye to me and hurried away, and I moved to shove two textbooks into my locker. The hallways had already thinned out; the bell would ring any moment now.

"Sooo..."

I turned in the direction of the new voice to see Christine Goddard leaning against the locker next to mine. She looked smug.

"Hi," I said, simply. "Was there something you wanted?"

"Nice open conversation in the hallway," she complimented. "I learned a lot. Really helped put the puzzle pieces together, you know?"

My heart dropped when I realized what she meant.

I'd let my guard down. Things had been so easy lately, what with losing the stress of faking a relationship and with things going so well with Sarah now. Jessa'd backed off of us, and we were so close to winning the crowns at Winter Formal. I should've known it was all too good to be true at this point, but for a moment, I'd truly thought Sarah and I were going to get out of this unscathed.

"The driver's license was bad, but I have to admit I wasn't expecting this," Christine remarked coolly. "I just figured she was cheating on you."

"You knew they were sleeping together, and that didn't strike you as something you should talk to your own boyfriend about?"

"I don't care what Sam does," Christine shot back. "I really don't. I just want that crown, and he's popular enough to help me win it."

"Aiming high," I complimented, my voice dripping with sarcasm. She leaned in closer to me and lowered her voice.

"Everyone's gonna hate you and Sarah when they find out your relationship started out as a pathetic attempt at getting attention from Sam."

"Well..." I hesitated, and then shut my locker. "It's real now. You're a little late."

"I don't think I am. Because if you two win those crowns, I'll tell everyone the truth. And you can say goodbye to all your new queer friends." The bell rang, and she smirked at me and then stalked off, leaving a lump in my throat in her place.

I sat down with Sarah in my next class, and she immediately noticed something was off. "Are you okay?"

"We need to talk," I hissed, and swallowed hard.

"Is there anything we can do about this?" I paced back in forth in Sarah's bedroom, fists clenched at my side.

"I mean... she knows. I don't think there's anything we can do about *that*."

"God, I'm such a screw up," I groaned out. "We were finally done with all of this. We were together, and things were so close to not being complicated anymore. We could've kept our friends and stayed in LAMBDA and did all of the things we said we were going to with them. It's ruined now."

"It's not ruined. Look, I've screwed up way more than you have. Remember me accidentally doing things that made Jessa suspicious? And actually being the one to let her know the truth?"

"Okay, but Christine is worse than Jessa. So much worse. She has no reason to keep this to herself."

"Yeah, she does. She gave you her reason: she wants to win the crown tomorrow."

"So? We can't control everyone's vote, Sarah."

"We could drop out." She looked to me and shrugged her shoulders. "I mean, if you wanted to."

"And do that to LAMBDA?"

"I guess so." She shrugged again. "I don't really want to, but..."

"If we do that, we lose them," I pointed out. "And Jessa might tell everyone the truth anyway."

"*Might.* But if we don't drop out, we probably lose them anyway, thanks to Christine. And we lose everyone else."

"Maybe... maybe if we just..." I tried, and then exhaled loudly when I came up empty.

"Katie, I don't think there's a right answer here. We can drop out last-minute and risk Jessa, or we can stay in the running and hope for a loss. If we lose, we lose. Maybe Jessa keeps her promise and doesn't say anything. And if we win... then we win."

"And Christine tells everyone everything," I acknowledged.

Sarah shrugged her shoulders again. She looked thoughtful now. "Well... not necessarily."

"How? If we win, she's telling. We're not going to change her mind."

"But she doesn't have to be the one to tell," Sarah pointed out. "*We* could. *I* could. I'm the one that started it."

"For the last time, you're not taking all of the blame here," I sighed out.

"Okay. I won't. But I could do the talking. Maybe if our friends hear it from me it'll soften the blow. Maybe I can explain it all."

"What, and they forgive us since we actually wound up gay?" I asked. "That hardly makes what we did any better. I mean, Jessa can think one thing but that doesn't mean everyone else will agree."

"Hey, if Jessa's cool with us now, I bet anyone could be," Sarah joked. "I mean... it's worth a try?"

"So that's it," I said. "We don't drop out?"

"Is that what you want?" she asked.

I stood in silence for a moment, thinking. I couldn't envision a scenario where dropping out made everything right again. LAMBDA would have a lot of questions. And besides... I kind of wanted to win. "Yes. Let's stay in. It's the right thing to do."

"You wanna kick Christine's ass," she replied, a knowing look in her eyes.

"That too."

Winter Formal wasn't as big as Prom, but it was pretty damn close. People grouped up and packed into limos all over Flowery Branch, and at eight o'clock sharp, we all entered a gym full of refreshments, balloons, and blaring stereos. A stage sat at one end of the gym, and a lone mic rested front and center.

Sarah and I went with a few of the LAMBDA kids in her car, with the promise to meet Dina, Josephine, and the others at the dance. As we arrived, Jake pointed to the stage and grinned. "That's where your crowning moment will take place, ladies."

"If we win," I reminded him.

"Are you kidding? You'll win," Hattie cut in, patting us both on the back. "Enjoy your night; I'm making Jake dance."

"Oh, God," Jake mumbled, but let Hattie pull him away nonetheless. Sarah and I shared a grin, and she guided me toward the refreshments.

"You look so pretty," she told me. "I love that dress on you. Blue is so your color."

"You literally dragged me to the mall and picked it out for me," I reminded her. "But you did a good job."

She grinned at me and then turned away to pour us two cups of punch, and I eyed her while she was distracted. She was gorgeous. Her hair was up in a bun with small ringlets hanging down to frame her face, and her dress was a sea foam color that worked perfectly with her skin tone. I hadn't been able to keep from staring at her back in her car.

"Here you go," she said, handing me my drink. "I don't know if it's been spiked, but I'm kind of hoping it has. I could use the liquid courage tonight."

"God." I looked around at our classmates out on the dance floor and grimaced. "They could all hate us by the end of the night."

"Not all of them. Just the ones with any respect for gay people."

"But remember: It's okay to fake it if you actually end up gay in the end," I joked.

"Right? Good luck to us."

"More like RIP our social lives," I corrected, and she touched the lip of her plastic cup to mine. We both took a long drink, and then Sarah set her cup down, took mine away, and then trashed it and led me to the dance floor. I pulled a face. "I don't dance."

"Liar," she retorted, and pulled me closer.

"Hey! Katie and Sarah!" That was Connor, naturally. He barged into our dance, half-drunk already, and was soon joined by an apologetic Graham and Bonnie and a laughing Dina and Josephine.

"Where's Hannah?" Sarah asked them.

"Flirting, of course," Dina replied. "She said she'd find us later. So, unfortunately, it seems we have an odd number here. Let's see... if Sarah and Katie pair off, and then one of us unlucky girls dances with Connor-"

"Hey!"

"-and another gets Graham... we still have an extra girl who needs a boy to pair off with."

"We'll switch off," Graham suggested. "I'll start with-"

"Actually," Bonnie cut in, drawing our attention to her, "...I'm gay. So I think I might find a girl to go dance with." She forced a smile, waved goodbye, and then she was gone. The rest of us stood in the center of the dance floor, stunned into silence. I exchanged a look with Connor and realized we were thinking the same thing: Our lunch table was quite the statistical anomaly.

"Well," Dina said at last, recovering. "Um... I didn't see that coming, but since Bonnie's busy, looks like this'll work out. I call Graham." She grabbed his hand before Josephine could argue, and, grudgingly, Josephine settled in front of

Connor, who smirked as he took her hand. I looked back to Sarah, who seemed distracted.

"Bonnie, though. Who would've thought?" she asked.

I let out a chuckle. "Come here. We don't have much time left."

And we didn't. Half an hour into the dance, Principal Crenshaw called for silence, and stood in the center of the stage, the mic in front of him. "Could all of our nominees for King and Queen please come to the stage, please."

"Ready for this?" Sarah whispered to me.

"Not really," I murmured, but gripped her hand and followed her nonetheless.

Chapter Fifteen

So here we were. The official winners of our school's Winter Formal crowns. And there Sarah was, explaining everything. A cold chill had settled over the crowd and I hadn't stopped feeling queasy since she'd started. I was almost thankful now that Sarah's speech seemed to be coming to an end.

"I can't express how truly sorry I am. How sorry *we* are. And... I get that the fact that I'm in love with her now doesn't change what my intentions were when this started. I know for some of you guys that may not be enough. And if that's the case, I understand. But..." she trailed off, and I heard her let out a shaky breath. "I have learned *so much* from this experience, and I want the members of

LAMBDA especially to know that. I understand what it's like for you to go to this school every day and feel like you're out of place, like you don't belong. I wouldn't wish that feeling on anyone, and you don't deserve it. Any of it. And for that reason, and because I fell in love, I wouldn't change any of it. I'd do it all over again, and I mean that in the most sincerest of ways, I swear. I just hope you guys can all forgive us for lying. I'm sorry. Katie's sorry."

She stepped back from the microphone to total silence, and moved to hand it to our stunned principal. But I rushed forward abruptly and took it instead with a prompt, "Wait."

Confused, Sarah handed me the microphone instead. I turned and faced the crowd, and immediately felt my cheeks heating up. I took a deep breath. "Um... hi. Look, I, um..." I trailed off, sucked in another breath, and forced myself to relax. "Okay, I don't want to get preachy here, because we all know it's lame and we shut down as soon as we hear it. Like, yes, we tried to do something good here."

I paused. "But... I think that the biggest thing I learned from all of this is that people are people. When I joined LAMBDA, I had some expectations about what the people there would be like. We all stereotype, you know? But that wasn't the case with them, and it's usually not the case with anyone else. And, I mean, the people I eat lunch with every day? Three months ago I thought I couldn't tell them anything. I thought every conversation we had would always be shallow. But I was wrong. They surprised me. People can surprise you. The kid you helped when he was getting picked on could wind up being one of your best friends. Even if he *is* gay. We're all human."

I glanced to Sarah as I continued, and she shot me an encouraging smile. "I love a girl. That's one part of me. I'm sorry that I hurt people by lying about my relationship with Sarah. But, like her, I'm not sorry I did it. I think we could all learn a lot about each other by spending three months in the shoes of someone gay. Thanks."

I turned away and shoved the microphone into Crenshaw's hands, then hissed to Sarah, "Okay, let's get out of here before we get killed."

"One second," she whispered back, then took her crown off and crossed the stage to Christine, who looked less than enthused by our little speeches. "Here's your dumb crown," Sarah snapped, shoving it points-up into her arms.

"Ow!" Christine exclaimed, glaring at her. Sarah ignored her and spun to face me, then took my hand and led me back down to the gym floor.

We wound our way through the murmuring crowd, all of whom didn't take their eyes off of us, and although I was eager to just leave, there was one thing I wanted to do more.

Sarah read my mind. We ducked in between clusters of people and made our way toward the left side of the gym, where, at last, we stopped in front of Jake. Sarah let go of my hand, and he and I made eye contact for what felt like minutes. I couldn't read his expression. At last, I forced myself to speak.

"I'm sorry," I said. "I should've been honest with you. I wish I had. I wish I'd just told you everything and... and maybe things could've been different. Maybe you'd have hated me, but maybe you wouldn't have and I could've gotten advice from you about what I was feeling, because I really was confused for a while. You're... you're kind of one of my best friends now, and I really don't want to lose that. I don't wanna lose any of you guys."

I fell silent, and winced as his eyes coldly searched mine. He opened his mouth, and I prepared for the worst.

"So... that first kiss in Room 405 is kind of hilarious in retrospect, now," he murmured. I look up at him, not daring to smile, and the corners of his mouth quirked upward. "Isn't it?"

"I saw Jesus for the first time that day," Sarah replied before I could, a matching smile on her lips. "Did not expect that at all, that's for sure."

"You two are definitely assholes," Jake told us. But then he shrugged his shoulders. "But you're gay assholes, and you're going to do a lot of activism to make it up to us, so I can forgive you."

"Thank you," I mouthed, and let him pull me in for a hug.

Two Weeks Later:

"This seat taken?"

I looked up from my spot on the bench on my front porch to see Sarah staring down at me. She was wearing a thin coat and shorts, and I marveled at her.

"You're insane. It's freezing!"

"Just as insane as you. Who reads outside in this weather? It's supposed to snow this week."

"I've only been out here for a couple of minutes," I explained, setting my book aside. "I'm waiting for Austin to come over."

"Austin?" Sarah looked taken aback. "Should I be jealous? Who *else* have you been meeting behind my back over Winter Break?"

"Oh, just the usual. Hattie, Dina, Josephine... Jessa invited me over for a threesome with Violet, but I told her I was all booked up."

"Wait, Jessa and Violet are dating?"

"No, I just threw two names out that made sense. You know, though, a little birdy told me Jake's got something going on with a guy."

"No way! Who?"

"Can't say. I'll just tell you that it's someone you know quite well."

"Henry?"

"Nope. This guy's not in LAMBDA."

"Well, given that no one really talks to us anymore other than the LAMBDA kids and our lunch group, that narrows it down to Graham and Connor."

"It would seem that way," I agreed, wiggling my eyebrows at her.

"Okay, now I know you're messing with me. Just tell me who it really is, seriously."

"Nope."

"Okay, well... at least tell me why Austin's coming over."

"I'm meeting his new girlfriend. He and I are trying this weird thing called friendship, and I hear that's what friends do, so."

"Well, you could use more friends," she joked, "given that most of the school doesn't like us anymore."

"True," I admitted. The homophobic kids hated us anyway, the really gay-friendly kids mostly looked down on us now, and the few who'd taken pity on us were already friends with us in the first place. The rest simply didn't care enough to strike up a friendship with us anymore than they had before. We'd kept all of our friends from before the Winter Formal drama, which was what we'd really hoped for, although Bonnie'd been a little understandably cold. It turns out we were the reason she'd been inspired to come out, so learning that we'd been living a lie for several months before genuinely dating had rubbed her the wrong way. But things were okay. We'd survive.

"I hear Brett Larson got a girl pregnant," I said, just making conversation. "Lesbian bonus: We can't do that."

Sarah burst into laughter next to me and recited, "Ninety-nine lesbian problems but a pregnancy ain't one. Nice."

"Did you just 'nice' your own joke?"

"Totally."

"...Nice."

She laughed again and shifted closer, resting her head on my shoulder. Her breath was visible on her next exhale, and I followed it as it floated through the air toward the front door. "So does your book have a happy ending?" she asked me. "The one you're reading?"

"That would require me to finish it first. But I doubt it; it's a crime thriller about a serial killer."

"No lesbians?"

"Of course there are lesbians. Every piece of media I consume now must have lesbians. This is how lesbianism works."

"So do they wind up together?"

"Well, one of them's the killer's first victim, so signs point to no."

She let out another visible breath, this time in the form of a quiet sigh.

"God dammit."

End

About the Author

Siera Maley was born and raised in the southern Bible Belt, where there wasn't much room for open-mindedness or diversity. After coming out as a lesbian as a teen, she relocated to a more suburban area and is now working on a four-year degree while living with her girlfriend and very adorable dog.